A R

A Riot of Goldfish

Kanoko Okamoto

Translated by J. Keith Vincent

ET REMOTISSIMA PROPE

Hesperus Worldwide

Hesperus Worldwide
Published by Hesperus Press Limited
4 Rickett Street, London sw6 1ru
www.hesperuspress.com

A *Riot of Goldfish* first published in Japanese as *Kingyo ryōran* in 1937
'The Food Demon' first published in Japanese as *Shokuma* in 1941

A *Riot of Goldfish* taken from *Kingyo: The Artistry of Japanese Goldfish* by
Kazuya Takaoka and Sachiko Kuru, published by Kodansha International Ltd.
English language translation © Kodansha International Ltd., 2004
Reprinted by permission. All rights reserved.

Introduction and English language translation of *The Food Demon*
© J. Keith Vincent, 2010

Foreword © David Mitchell, 2010

Designed and typeset by Fraser Muggeridge studio
Printed in Jordan by Jordan National Press

ISBN: 978-1-84391-852-3

Contents

Foreword

Okamoto Kanoko was born Ōnuki Kano in 1889 into a wealthy Tokyo family, and spent a childhood of privilege and ill-health in nearby Kawasaki. She is bracketed by Donald Keene, the eminent critic of Japanese letters, amongst a group of women writers who cut their literary teeth in the 1930s – the first decade since the Heian Age of Murasaki Shikibu and Sei Shōnagon nine centuries earlier that permitted women to compete for literary glory.

Whilst many of her contemporaries drew material from the ideological battles of the age, Okamoto is more concerned with themes of aesthetics and the artist than with class consciousness, female liberation or the politics of the expanding Japanese empire. Mataichi the goldfish breeder from 'A Riot of Goldfish' determines to 'unleash a gorgeous ethereal creation into the water, a creation made – unlike painting, sculpture, or architecture – from the stuff of life itself'. The narrative traces his career from awkward foster-son to aquaculture researcher to misanthropic recluse, tracking along the way the life cycle of obsession. (Thematic turf, coincidentally, well staked-out in the thirties by the youthful Tanizaki Juni'chiro, a classmate of Okamoto's brother, and thinly veiled presence in her first story to win popular acclaim, *The Dying Crane*, a story about yet another writer, Akutagawa Ryūnosuke.) The genesis of Mataichi's life-long quest is convincingly banal: an unrequited love for his classmate and his patron's daughter, Masako, whose approval the young man is desperate to earn. When she marries another man, Mataichi sublimates his longing for her into his quest for a goldfish of unprecedented beauty, but in time the obsession acquires its own momentum and, finally, subsumes his life. In one lucid passage, Mataichi even suspects that 'it was not human beings who made goldfish, but... the goldfish themselves [that] had continued doggedly towards their goal by seducing and exploiting the weakest of human instincts – that that is driven by beauty.' Okamoto chooses dialogue and imagery that allude to her overall theme: Teizō, Mataichi's patron, confesses, 'to put it bluntly, in my family there's just one female goldfish. So when I see a male, I can't help feeling a little envious and wanting to help out.' Elsewhere, cities swallow people whole; and Yoshie, his temporary lover, allows Mataichi to fold her 'like an invertebrate animal into whatever awkward position he liked'.

Some Japanese critics find Okamoto's style overwrought and her exemplary translator here, J. Keith Vincent, has not abused his position by removing blemishes of excess. In a story about a frustrated striving for aesthetic perfection, however, such a demerit is a merit of a kind. If the author does not worry about endowing her protagonist with likeability, this is simply because he is a dislikeable man: in the closing section, Mataichi becomes, in the words of the goldfish breeders he berates, 'a giant water-bug' that attacks their treasured fish; and several years slide away in a run of cold-blooded, world-weary sentences until the narrative reaches a strong and wistful finale.

The protagonist of 'The Food Demon', Besshirō, is as clever, manipulative and gnawed by existential doubts as Mataichi, but is also (for my money) better-fleshed with consistent in-consistencies: doubly important for a writer working in an environment where character and scenario counted for more than plot twists. Where Mataichi is a monomaniac in search of the perfect goldfish, Besshirō strives to enter the higher echelons first as a conventional artist: he submits to, rather than embraces, his true vocation as a chef, and remains wormy with self-doubt and bent under the sack of chips on his shoulder which his illegitimate birth bequeathed him. He resents his put-upon wife Itsuko's meekness, yet, all too realistically, she and their infant son will more than likely save her husband from himself. Besshirō can be spiteful and adolescent, but also tender and observant: 'As he worked he felt a rare flood of love and affection for other people. It was no longer about winning or losing... Wasn't cooking an act of love? And wasn't that love best spent on children and half-wits?'

The story's structure is correspondingly subtler: where the narrative of 'A Riot of Goldfish' follows a downward diagonal, 'The Food Demon' is a loop, beginning in Besshirō's present with his employer's two daughters, his walk home and a scene with his wife, before returning back in time to Besshirō's childhood and youth in Kyoto. The story trails loose ends, notably the relationship between Besshirō and his mother and adoptive father, but these loose ends feel like this impulsive and lurching young man's, rather than his creator's. Where the central relationship of 'A Riot of Goldfish' is a non-relationship, Besshirō falls in with an older man named Higaki, a restaurant owner, rake and artist who, like Okamoto, knows his Greenwich from his Greenwich Village. Agreeing that they were 'brought up among the lower classes by mistake', the two friends 'clung to art as the only means by which they could use their instincts to elevate themselves to their rightful place'. (The mish-mash milieu of imported European and American modernism and Japanese traditional values, which was con-structing the ideology that would soon present the world with Pearl Harbour, is well-portrayed and makes 'The Food Demon' well worth reading as a Taisho period piece.) Higaki on his opium-addled deathbed 'gives' his protégé a sole surviving relative in Tokyo. This aunt proves the conduit to the life in which we initially encounter Besshirō, working as a malcontent cookery teacher. Thus does 'The Food Demon' arrive back at its present, where the train of Besshirō's meditations during a hail-storm deliver a kind of peace.

The insightful critic (and underrated novelist) Maruya Saiichi observes that Okamoto's short fictions read as sketches for novels, and speculates that had she survived into her fifties and sixties and worked with the longer form, she could have bloomed into one of Japan's major twentieth-century writers. As it is, she must remain one of the many whose potential outshine their oeuvres. Twenty-first century reading tastes may find Okamoto Kanoko prolix and florid in some passages. Charges that she overestimates her own knowledge about how society's lower orders view the beautiful uplands would probably stick; accusations of snobbery would not trouble her; and the modern idea that writers should best wear their learning lightly would have provoked a bewildered 'Why?'. The same criticisms could be levelled at many European writers of the 1920s and 1930s, however, and although 'A Riot of Goldfish' and 'The Food Demon' are not flawlessly great works – very few novellas are – they do glint with greatness, amply justify Hesperus Press' lush reprint and underline the second adjective in Donald Keene's final verdict on Okamoto Kanoko: 'A minor, but unforgettable writer.'

– *David Mitchell, 2010*

Introduction

Okamoto Kanoko's career as a writer of fiction lasted only three years, from 1936 until her death in 1939 at the age of forty-nine. But during those years she wrote over a dozen short stories and novellas remarkable for their lush language, complex psychological portraits and frank sexuality that recalled the 'decadent' aestheticism of the 1920s. As an aesthete in a time of war, a cosmopolitan in a time of virulent nationalism, and an unrepentant narcissist in a time of mass mobilisation, Kanoko had plenty of detractors. But she had lots of fans as well. Critic Hayashi Fusao, writing in 1938 in an essay entitled 'The Rebirth of Japanese Literature', praised her style as equalling that of Mori Ōgai and Natsume Sōseki, the two towering greats of the Meiji period of 1868–1912. And future Nobel laureate Kawabata Yasunari was so moved by one of her stories about the Tōkaidō Highway that he famously took it with him on a trip to retrace the route taken by its protagonist.

Okamoto Kanoko was born in Tokyo in 1889 as the eldest daughter of a wealthy family from the village of Futago in what is now the city of Kawasaki, Japan. She was brought up mostly in the countryside under the care of a governess who had her memorise passages from the Japanese classics, such as *The Tale of Genji* and *The Pillow Book*, and taught her to compose poetry in the 31-syllable *waka* form. Later she attended the Atomi Gakuen, a progressive girls' school in Tokyo, and began to publish her poetry with the encouragement of the great feminist poet Yosano Akiko (1878–1942). In 1911 she joined Yosano, Hiratsuka Raichō, Tamura Toshiko and others as one of the first contributors to *Blue Stockings* (*Seitō*), an influential early feminist literary journal. Kanoko's poetry, like Akiko's, was a passionate celebration of the power of female sexuality. Her prose works, too, have a distinctly feminist edge. When Masako, for example, tells Mataichi in 'A Riot of Goldfish' that she is more excited to see the perfect goldfish he is breeding than the baby in her own womb, she is not only acting like a perfect aesthete, but also implicitly voicing her opposition to the appropriation of women's wombs by an increasingly militarised state.

In 1910 Kanoko married the impecunious but charming cartoonist Okamoto Ippei, who at first turned out to be a disaster as a husband. Once he finally began to earn a good income he spent it all carousing with geisha, leaving Kanoko and their infant son Tarō at home with barely enough to eat. But after a few years of this, Ippei realised the harm he was doing and made the decision, extraordinary for a man at the time, to dedicate the rest of his life to nurturing and supporting his wife in her career. When she told him in 1913 that she had found a young lover who made her happy, Ippei not only agreed to let her continue seeing him, but invited him to move into their home. The young man, whose name was Horikiri Naoto, died in 1916 after living with the couple for most of the final three years of his life, more than satisfying Kanoko, according to one account, thanks to a voracious sexual appetite that was thought to be particular to tubercular patients. This and many other interesting tidbits can be found in Setouchi Harumi's adoring biography of Kanoko, *Kanoko ryōran* (Kōdansha, 1971), the title of which happens to echo that of *A Riot of Goldfish* (*Kingyo ryōran*). After Horikiri's death Kanoko and Ippei devoted themselves to the study of religion, first Christianity and then Buddhism. She published widely on Buddhism during the 1920s and by the end of the decade was a recognised authority and much sought-after speaker on the subject. Readers will note that the 'female *waka* poet and scholar of Buddhism' and her husband for whom Besshirō cooks a meal towards the end of 'The Food Demon' bear a striking resemblance to Kanoko and Ippei.

In 1929 the Okamotos brought two more of Kanoko's male admirers with them and their son on a grand tour of Europe and America. By this point she and Ippei were famous enough that their departure by ship from Yokohama was given lavish coverage, complete with photographs, in the *Asahi shimbun*. They stayed away for almost three years, setting up residences in London, Paris, and Berlin, and Kanoko wrote dispatches back to Japanese journals on her impressions of Western culture. She was particularly interested in cuisine, and an essay she wrote shortly after her return to Japan in 1932, 'To the Gourmets' ('Gūrume ni okuru') would become the basis for 'The Food Demon'. It includes, among other things, the description of the Parisian restaurant Foyot that the couple in 'The Food Demon' relate to Besshirō. 'Gūrume ni okuru' was republished in 2009, together with 'The Food Demon', in an anthology of 'masterpieces of culinary literature' by Okamoto, which suggests that her work is enjoying something of a boom in Japan at present. *Shokuma: Okamoto Kanoko shokubungaku kessakushū* is published by Kōdansha Bungei Bunko.

Kanoko had informed Ippei in 1919 that their marriage would henceforth be a celibate one, apparently believing that conjugal sexuality was deadening to the spirit of an artist. But there were always other men in her life. The two admirers who accompanied them to Europe continued living with the Okamotos upon their return. One served as her personal physician and helped the other with the cooking and cleaning, while Ippei served as research assistant and secretary. Kanoko, who was always utterly convinced of her own value and importance, took these tributes as perfectly natural, and while many critics, both male and female, found this lifestyle scandalous, others have pointed out that she was simply living the way many men would with a wife, maid, and mistress. In her fiction she endowed many of her female characters with the same ability to hold men under their sway. Masako in 'A Riot of Goldfish' and Okinu in 'The Food Demon' are good examples of typical Okamoto heroines who share their author's magnetism.

Like Mataichi with his goldfish and Besshirō in the kitchen, Kanoko was passionately devoted to her craft as a writer. As a student of Buddhism and classical literature she had an enormous vocabulary in Japanese and Chinese that she was never shy of flaunting, while her familiarity with European novels led her to push against the boundaries of what was possible in literary Japanese at the time. She was particularly adept at capturing subtle shifts of mood and atmosphere. The narrative voice in her texts shifts easily in and out of the minds of her characters in a way that is reminiscent of the work of Higuchi Ichiyō (1872–1896) and Murasaki Shikibu (c. 970–c. 1031) before her. But while Ichiyō and Lady Murasaki wrote in classical Japanese, whose vagueness in terms of person and tense makes such blurring of boundaries almost inevitable, Kanoko manages the same effect in crisp modern Japanese. In the extraordinary scene in which Besshirō feasts on daikon in the main room of his borrowed house while his timid wife Itsuko listens apprehensively from the next room, we move back and forth between the consciousness of husband and wife with as much ease as the sounds of clinking dishes that penetrate the paper door.

As in much of the best Japanese fiction, not much happens in either of the two stories in this volume, and what does happen tends to have more to do with atmosphere and character than an unfolding plot. When decisive events do occur, like the moment in 'A Riot of Goldfish' when the last cherry blossom petal sticks in the back of Mataichi's throat or when Besshirō in 'The Food Demon' tosses the endives in the trash, they have an overdetermined quality, like what Freud called 'screen memories', singled out as a symbolic amalgam of past experience. At the same time, iterative evocations of the past shift suddenly into the narration of unique events, which has the effect of transforming the flow of time into an accumulation of images. Everything seems to be over and done with before the stories even begin, so the point for the reader is not to find out what will happen, but to understand what *has* happened to make the characters who they are. The result is to quiet desire and dampen agency while promoting in the reader a serene sense of detachment, as if to say with a sigh, as Besshirō does when he looks back on his life, 'That's all there was to it.' Of course the male protagonists Mataichi and Besshirō are driven by desire and ambition, but the narrative stands back and observes them calmly as they flail about. The women, on the other hand, become weirdly empowered by the same spectacle. This is classic Kanoko: her female characters seem to draw their energy from the men while the men struggle like flies in ointment.

About the Translation

This translation of 'A Riot of Goldfish' was first published by Kodansha International in 2004, in a book otherwise devoted to gorgeous images of Japanese goldfish: *Kingyo: The Artistry of Japanese Goldfish*. As a story about its protagonist's obsession with goldfish, this was a perfect home for it. But I am thrilled that Hesperus has agreed to republish it here along with 'The Food Demon', another story of a man obsessed, but this time with food. 'The Food Demon' appears here in translation for the first time.

As for the translations themselves, there are a couple of things I would like to mention. The name of the character Mataichi in 'A Riot of Goldfish' is usually read 'Fukuichi', and most commentators in English have chosen this reading. I made the unorthodox choice of 'Mataichi' to emphasise the meaning of the name, which is something like 'once again', or 'one more time'. Also, if we read the first character of Mataichi's name as 'Mata' rather than 'Fuku', the first line of the story begins with what in Japanese is called a '*kakekotoba*', or 'pivot word', in which syllables are meant to be read twice. Thus the opening phrase, '*Kyō mo* Mata*ichi*,' can be read, 'Today *again*, Mataichi,' even though the word 'Mata' (again) is used only in the name. This sort of poetic flourish is typical of Kanoko and also rather nicely encapsulates the story's preoccupation with repetition and agency.

The title 'The Food Demon' is a direct translation of Kanoko's Japanese title (*Shokuma*), but another possible rendering of it would be 'The Gourmet'. While the term 'gourmet' (rendered phonetically in Japanese as *gurume*) is quite common in Japanese today, it was not yet known to Japanese in the 1930s and Kanoko coined her own term to translate it after encountering it in France, using the Chinese characters for 'food' and 'demon'. As I mentioned earlier, the first iteration of 'The Food Demon' was an essay that used this word in the title. But while in the earlier essay she glossed the Chinese characters as *gurume*, in the present story she leaves them unglossed, which suggests that she meant to emphasise the actual meaning of the characters rather than simply use them to translate 'gourmet'. There is, after all, something demonic about Besshirō the gourmet.

'A Riot of Goldfish' was first published in the journal *Chūō Kōron* in 1937 and 'The Food Demon' was published posthumously in 1941, in a volume that incidentally included two other stories dealing with food, 'Sushi' and 'The House Spirit'. Both 'Sushi' and 'The House Spirit' have been translated, along with several others of Kanoko's best works, by Kazuko Sugizaki in *The House Spirit and Other Stories*, Capra Press, 1995. For this translation I have used the versions of both stories published in her collected works, *Okamoto Kanoko zenshū*, Tōjusha, 1974. Both stories are also available online at aozora.gr.jp

For an excellent and more detailed discussion of Kanoko's life and works see Maryellen T. Mori, *The Splendor of Self-Exaltation: The Life and Fiction of Okamoto Kanoko*, in *Monumenta Nipponica*, vol. 50, no. 1 (spring 1995) pp. 67–102.

Finally, I would like to thank Yoshiharu Muto who, as always, was enormously helpful to me during the translation of 'A Riot of Goldfish' and Hiromi Miyagi-Lusthaus who was just as helpful when it came time to translate 'The Food Demon'. They went over every word of these stories and helped me sort out some very thorny passages. Many thanks as well to Alice Albinia at Hesperus Press, whose enthusiasm for Okamoto's work made this translation possible, and to Ellie Robins for a fine job of copy editing.

– *J. Keith Vincent*, 2010

A Riot of Goldfish

Today again Mataichi scooped the tiny fish one by one into a shallow bowl and examined them carefully under a magnifying glass. Their colours had finally begun to change, but it looked as if he had failed this year as well. Once more he had failed to breed the goldfish he had hoped for. Mumbling his disappointment, he tossed the bowl and the magnifying glass onto the veranda and flopped down blank-faced with a thud.

From his vantage point on the veranda, he could see that the new leaves in the ravine were at their peak. The treetops, freshly green and yet more showy than leaves alone should be, were enlivened by a bouquet of overtones ranging from reddish brown to youthful hues of purple. As the trees swayed gently in the breeze, the smooth red clay of the cliff beyond shone like a golden screen. The cliff stood fifty feet high or more and was dotted here and there with *kirishima* azaleas.

From the shadows of the bamboo grove at the base of the cliff grew a patch of moist grass with late primroses and early nasturtiums blooming profusely all the way to the bank of a small stream. The stream flowed with water from a spring in the ravine and was essential to the livelihood of a goldfish breeder like Mataichi. Seven or eight goldfish ponds were fed with water diverted from the stream. Some of these were covered with reed screens and others were left open to the air. Opposite the cliff, water roared along a large ditch at the foot of the stone wall beside the road. It was turbid sewer water from the city.

Six years ago, when Mataichi had returned from the provincial experimental fisheries station to take over the goldfish business from his adoptive parents, the late spring flowers had also been blooming in the ravine.

Mataichi had grown up in this place until he left for the fisheries school as a young man, but on returning to it now he realised for the first time how extraordinary it was that such a paradise should exist right in the middle of Tokyo. He had been thrilled to be running the goldfish shop that occupied this valley. But six years later the same gentle scenery and the sound of the water could only further parch his now stony heart. He lifted his expressionless eyes to the top of the cliff.

A semicircular chapel in the Romanesque style stood in one corner of the imposing garden, whose lawn drooped over the cliff's edge. Each of the chapel's round columns stood out against the high blue sky, casting vivid lavender and rose-coloured shadows in the June sun. Beyond them white clouds could be seen slowly moving across the sky as if stepping from column to column.

Today Masako from the big house on the cliff could be seen seated as usual in the middle of the semicircular chapel, her ample figure thrust forward to receive the sun on her chest. Even at this distance, Mataichi could see a tangle of yarn, with which she had begun to knit something, covering her lap, and also on her lap a baby girl was sprawled, nodding off to sleep. It was a picture of happiness and could not have been further from the way Mataichi was feeling. Masako was quite short-sighted and so probably could not see him. Since Mataichi saw her like this every day, it was not a vision that moved him particularly. And yet things had come to the point that nothing moved or stopped Mataichi's heart unless he tried to stir up some emotion, be it of jealousy, envy, or lingering attachment, in relation to this vision.

'Must I be subjected to this again today?' thought Mataichi. 'She parades through life as if I didn't exist. And it's my fate never to be able to forget her.'

Mataichi got up suddenly and lit a cigarette.

Back then Masako, who was known as 'the young Miss from the big house on the cliff', was a rather inconspicuous young girl. She rarely spoke, tended to stare at the ground, and had

4

a habit of biting her lip. An only child who had lost her mother at an early age and had been brought up by her father, one might well have thought her a melancholy little girl. Nonetheless, she did not appear to dwell particularly on one thought more than any other and showed only the most sluggish reactions to worldly stimuli. When she came alone to Mataichi's carrying a bucket to buy goldfish and was chased by a puppy on her way back home, for all her panic she moved too slowly. But once she made up her mind to escape, she would run to a much further distance than was necessary, where she would finally relax and display a delayed look of terror in her eyes. Her artless round eyes and peculiar movements made Mataichi's adoptive father, Sōjūrō, chuckle and liken her to a *ranchū* goldfish, although he made a point of not saying it too loudly, since she was the daughter of one of his best customers.

Out of a vague sense of class antagonism, the family who ran the goldfish business at the foot of the cliff felt a certain resentment towards the inhabitants of the big house on top of the cliff, so the parents did not bother to berate Mataichi when he joined other neighbourhood kids picking on Masako on the way to and from elementary school. Whenever a maid from the house on the cliff came down to complain, they made a show of apologising, but as soon as she left they said not a word to Mataichi and acted as if it was someone else's problem.

Thanks to this attitude on the part of his family, Mataichi's perverse tormenting of Masako gradually escalated. He dogged her with comments impugning her chastity that belied his young years.

'I saw you get the gym teacher to reach under your arms and pull up your pants. He's a man, you know! You nasty girl!'

'You ran up to that boy with the nosebleed and gave him two tissues, didn't you? I know what you're up to!'

And he always ended by telling her, 'You're hopeless. A girl like you will never find a husband.'

These comments invariably plunged Masako into a despair she thought would never go away. Her face would drain of all colour as she stared fixedly at Mataichi. Her large, downcast eyes revealed only bewilderment, without a trace of malice or defiance. It was as if she were allowing the pain caused by the sharp thorns of his words to fill her heart until it overflowed as tears. Soon her face would tremble violently and a single, pearl-coloured tear would emerge from her lower eyelid like the rising moon. Masako would bring her sleeve to her eyes and quickly turn around.

Her back, rather broad for her age, would convulse in silence. As he watched, Mataichi felt the sudden dispersion of the alien mass of boyish sexuality that was trapped hot within him. In its place his breast filled with a sweet, lip-smacking sadness. Without any particular intention in mind, Mataichi played the adult and yelled at Masako, 'Act like a lady, you tomboy!'

And yet it seemed that Masako's love for goldfish was strong enough to make her brush off these incidents and keep coming back to Mataichi's to buy more. When his parents were home he never bullied her. Instead he would avert his gaze and whistle nonchalantly.

One spring evening Masako came walking by Mataichi's house, this time without a bucket. Mataichi spotted her immediately and started on his usual bullying. Filling with that sweet sadness, he spat out the usual, 'Act like a lady,' at Masako's back. But this time Masako surprised him by turning around to meet his glare. A sly smile broke out like a flesh-coloured slice of fig on her girlish, tear-drenched face, and she shot back, 'How exactly should I act like a lady?'

And no sooner had Mataichi time to be taken aback by these words than her fist shot out of her sleeve and opened to shower

6

him with a face full of cherry petals. 'How's that for ladylike?' – she said, hopping back slightly and then retreating in a burst of girlish giggles.

Mataichi thought he had closed his mouth immediately, but he could taste cool shreds of cherry petals in his mouth. He coughed and spat them out, but one remained lodged there, sticking to the soft part of the back of his throat, where he could not dislodge it either with the tip of his tongue or even by plunging his finger into his throat. Mataichi began to panic as he imagined himself choking to death and ran to the well in a torrent of tears. He gargled with well water and finally managed to spit out the last of the petals. But one painful petal remained behind in some unreachable region of his heart from where it would never be removed.

From then on, when Mataichi met Masako, he still thrust his shoulders back and maintained his outward dignity. But inside he felt utterly spineless. He could no longer say a word to her. For her part, Masako acted like a perfect grown-up and greeted him with studied politeness whenever they met. However, from that day on she sent a maid to buy her goldfish.

Masako and Mataichi – she from the mansion on top of the cliff and he from the goldfish shop in the ravine – began to attend separate high schools. The two had different friends and different interests and seldom saw each other. But on those rare occasions when they did cross paths, in the movie theatre or elsewhere, Mataichi saw that Masako was becoming so beautiful he could barely suppress his hostility. In her pouting, finely wrought face, her downcast eyes smouldered like black lacquer. Her lips curled up slightly at the corners in a provoking smile. The flesh of her newly acquired womanhood rose full from breast to shoulder, and her limbs stretched firm and graceful. When they met, Masako would straighten up like a lady and greet Mataichi with a superior look. He would wince and duck to one side, but he felt his ears burn with her attention. Masako's friends were asking her about him.

'He's the boy from the goldfish shop down from our house. He's very good in school.' Hearing nothing beyond the flattest explanatory tone in this comment, Mataichi blushed hot with shame.

Caught up in the economic crisis that followed the Great War, Mataichi and his family heard that Masako's family in the big house on the cliff had suffered a serious blow to their finances. But, looking up from below, one would never have guessed it from the way they were adding to the Western-style house and rebuilding the garden. They were also buying more goldfish from Mataichi's family. The maid who came for goldfish food told them, 'The master says now is the time to build since craftsmen's wages are cheaper.' It was also at this time that the semicircular Romanesque chapel went up on the edge of the cliff.

'If you can't have fun making money, you can at least try to enjoy life,' said Teizō, Masako's scrawny, dark-complexioned father, on a rare visit down from the cliff to inspect the goldfish ponds. He was a man of fifty, dressed casually in an understated *ichiraku* kimono and never without a pouch of stomach medicine in his sleeve. He quietly kept a mistress in separate quarters, but had never brought another woman into the family since he lost the beautiful young wife who had been Masako's mother and whom he had married for love. Something in his character made him enjoy this show of fidelity.

Teizō sat down on the veranda of Mataichi's house alongside the goldfish buckets that were leaning against it to dry and chatted with Mataichi's adoptive father, Sōjūrō. Sōjūrō's family goldfish business was one of the oldest in the valley, while Teizō's big house on the cliff was only fifteen or sixteen years old, built after they cleared away a paulownia grove the year before Masako was born.

And yet, for such a newcomer, Teizō was amazingly familiar with what went on in the neighbourhood, and with goldfish. His grandfather had lived in a similar valley in the central Yamanote area of Tokyo and was a great lover of goldfish. Naturally, building his home on a cliff above a goldfish shop brought Teizō memories of raising goldfish as a boy. The sense of cool detachment from the world that prevailed in Teizō after the loss of his beautiful, much-loved wife only intensified his fascination with the curious beauty of goldfish as living creatures that seemed more like objects than organisms.

'In the Edo period,' Teizō once expounded to Sōjūrō, 'raising goldfish was a respectable sideline for poor bannermen of the shogun. You could find goldfish ponds in most valleys in the high ground of Azabu and Akasaka in the Yamanote area, wherever water came out of the ground. Your place is one of them right?'

Sōjūrō, who was, after all, the specialist in goldfish, responded rather half-heartedly. 'I suppose so. In any case we've been at it for three or four generations.'

The lack of confidence in Sōjūrō's response, delivered as he stared up at the soot-stained ceiling, was much to be expected. Although he and his wife had raised Mataichi, they had actually been adopted into the family. They were a young couple descended from the family's vassals, and when both of Mataichi's parents fell ill and died while he was still nursing, relatives nominated Sōjūrō and his wife to raise the boy and take over the family business. Before that, they were rather unsuccessful instructors of traditional *ogiebushi* singing. Sōjūrō confessed to a strange anxiety about mucking around with living creatures when they first started out.

'Mataichi is the real head of this business so I suppose it's right that he should work with goldfish. But I'm not sure. Young people have their own ideas these days.' Sōjūrō spoke rather casually, with one eye on Mataichi, who was studying for an exam in the corner of the *tatami*-floored room.

'No. Goldfish are fine. Have him stick with it by all means. Garden variety goldfish don't fetch much, but if you can come up with new improved breeds, the sky's the limit. And these days there's quite a demand from foreigners. Goldfish breeding is a proper industry in Japan.'

Mataichi turned to listen, struck by how knowledgeable one had to be as an entrepreneur. Teizō went on, 'But you've got to be able to apply the latest scientific techniques. I don't mean to be rude, but if you folks can't afford to send Mataichi to a good school, I'm happy to help out with his tuition.'

Surprised by the suddenness of this proposal and the casual way in which it was made, Sōjūrō looked into the rich man's face. Teizō took a step back and explained himself. 'I mean, to put it bluntly, in my family there's just one female goldfish. So when I see a male, I can't help feeling a little envious and wanting to help out.'

Mataichi thought talking about people as male and female goldfish was a bit much even as a joke and felt a surge of annoyance. But another part of him knew that overcoming his habitual defiant attitude might be a way of getting closer to Masako. The bittersweet memory of the cherry petal thrown by Masako that stuck to the back of his mouth had him anxiously probing the area with his tongue again.

'It must worry you to have only one daughter,' said Sōjūrō's wife as she served tea. But Teizō replied with a sudden optimistic resolve, 'At least I'm free to go out and find a good male and make him my son-in-law. If it's your own son, you're stuck with him even if he's an idiot.'

In the end, Teizō's proposal was accepted and Mataichi was set to attend a higher technical school to study goldfish breeding, with Teizō subsidising his tuition. Masako acted as if she knew nothing of the situation. But before he knew it there were indeed three of those young males Teizō was so desirous of helping out hanging around Masako in their gold-buttoned uniforms, coming and going and generally making a nuisance of themselves to Mataichi. As far as he could make out, Masako treated each of them with equal affection. Teizō was a self-made man who did not feel that paying people's tuition gave him any special authority over them, and he used the young men simply as conversation partners. Their names were Tomoda, Haritani, and Yokochi, and they seemed to have been chosen on the single condition that they be free of obsequiousness. Consequently, they all shared a casual air towards the daughter of the family that was paying their tuition, rapping her playfully with their tennis racquets and calling her by her first name, as they would any other young woman. The effect was to camouflage completely from their consciousness and others' the fact that they were three male rivals for the affection of a single female. This probably made it easier for Masako to treat them equally as well.

Watching this polished and jovial social scene as it played itself out among the young people in the mansion on the cliff, Mataichi felt his own personality pulling him in the opposite direction, however unfortunate he knew it to be. He wondered why anyone would want to spend time with such a spineless bunch and knew he could never engage in such a half-hearted courtship. For him it was conquer or be conquered. But recently he felt Masako's beauty and its effect on him reaching extraordinary heights. Such beauty in the object of his love and affection was fast making her the kind of woman whose mere presence could sap all the strength out of a young man like Mataichi, whose confrontational style made it impossible for him to rest until he locked horns with his competitors. It was around this time that the precocious young man's mind began to fasten on thoughts of life's dilemmas and an assortment of more perverse notions. In the end he resolved not to set foot on top of the cliff and to resist Masako with his own special brand of obstinacy. Mataichi knew that for someone like himself, whose only asset was strength devoid of polish or panache, any attempt to mix with the crowd up there could only end in ignominious defeat. Next to a goddess like Masako, Mataichi was certainly out of his league. In her company he could only be a cowardly buffoon or an overbearing boor. His first inclination was to act aggrieved, whatever the cost. Under normal circumstances Masako would never be his. But spitefully pursuing the only path open to him might just get her attention. Mataichi gradually lost himself in those sad sweet memories of perversely tormenting her as a boy.

Before long, Mataichi graduated from high school and became a research student at a fisheries station with an emphasis on domesticated fish located on the shore of a lake in the Kansai region. One September evening, a week before his scheduled departure, Masako came down from the cliff shining a flashlight to deliver travel money from her father and her own parting gift for Mataichi. Having accepted expressions of thanks from Sōjūrō and his wife, Masako said to Mataichi, 'Shall we go for tea in the Ginza before you go?'

At these words, spoken so casually as Masako straightened her obi, Mataichi felt the bottom drop out of his stubborn resolve. But he was not giving up yet.

'Ginza is a bit crowded and noisy. But I might be persuaded to go to Enoki-chō.'

Mataichi's way of speaking to Masako had changed in the last three or four years. Gradually he had adopted a mode of expression that was too formal for friends and more suited to a young man and woman of slightly disparate status.

'Strange place for a walk. But it's fine with me. Enoki-chō it is.'

Running diagonally between the spacious hubbub of Akasaka Sannōshita and the dense chaos of Roppongi's Aoi-chō, Enoki-chō was a charming night district packed with modest shop-fronts displaying a good selection of products that changed frequently. The light from the store lanterns was perfect for early autumn, preserving just the right amount of darkness on the streets as it sparkled and flowed in puddles on the ground. On the planks in the gutters in front of fruit stalls, leftover water-melons lay in dark green piles like stray cannonballs, while pride of place in the display windows went to Asian pears and grapes that had just come into season. A fat girl sat on a folding stool looking through a picture book. It was a quaint little street, not too noisy and not too quiet.

Taxis rarely ventured there, so Masako and Mataichi were free to stroll side by side down the middle of the street. He had not been this close to her in six or seven years. At first, her grown-up woman's body seemed to ooze so much sensuality that he wanted to cover his skin in a suit of armour lest the slightest undulation on her part should topple his sense of sexual independence. But soon he felt something dissolve within him, and before he knew it he was ripping the armour off himself and happily floating inside the confines of her aura. Suddenly the store lanterns and the crowds took on a sensuous blur, as if he were seeing them through a cloud of perfume, and his self-consciousness finally faded away.

But some resistance still smouldering inside him caused him to drop two or three paces behind Masako. He believed he had an objective view of Masako and himself. His eyes moved from the tidy Irish lace lining her slightly pulled-back collar to the hollow in her perfectly cylindrical neck and on to those gentle mounds of flesh rising like newly pounded *mochi*.

'She has developed all the physical charms a woman could want,' thought Mataichi with a quiet sigh. He was much taller than Masako. Mataichi hated himself for his inability to keep from staring at her and turned his head to the side to distract himself from the sadness caused by such an unattainable object. His line of sight found refuge in the shadowy shrine grounds of Sannō no Mori at the end of a small alleyway.

'Mataichi, are you really set on going into the goldfish business?' Masako asked casually, turning to the side where she thought Mataichi was. Mataichi was one step behind but hurried to catch up.

'I wouldn't mind doing something more interesting, but things aren't that easy.'

'That's no kind of attitude! If I were you I would love to raise goldfish.' Masako's features seemed to blur and melt into her most serious expression. 'It's none of my business really, but I think goldfish are the freest and the most beautiful creatures people can make.'

Mataichi had a funny feeling. Up until then, the only intelligence he had sensed in Masako seemed little more than a form of social grace bred from the easy luxury in which she had been raised. But here she was making a critical pronouncement on life values. Was this something that had just occurred to her during their walk, or was it something to which she had given some thought?

'That might be true, but they're just goldfish after all.'

At this, Masako's distracted expression was intensified by pupils that seemed to smoulder with emphasis.

'You might be the son of a breeder but you don't really understand the value of goldfish. People have lived and died for goldfish, you know.'

Masako started on a story, which she said she had heard from her father. Having grown up in the goldfish business, Mataichi knew the story even better than she. And yet in her retelling, vague though it was, it seemed to reverberate with greater

14

meaning. The story went something like this. Around 1895, after the Sino-Japanese War, goldfish fever reached a peak. Specialists in the industry took the opportunity to form associations, and they even made attempts to export goldfish to America. The most progressive among them tried to stimulate demand by crossing different breeds to come up with curious new ones. The famous breeder Akiyama in the Sunamura district of Tokyo took the magnificent fleshy lump from the head of the *ranchū* and combined it with the supple curves and billowing tail of the *ryūkin* to create an exquisite new breed that would be perfect from head to tail. After eight years of near miraculous efforts, heaping refinement upon refinement, he finally achieved his goal. The birth of this famous fish, called the *shūkin,* belonged to the chaotic early days of the goldfish boom.

Soon there were enormous numbers of enthusiastic amateur breeders. They held competitions and published rankings of the most beautiful fish. Given the cost of the equipment, the social obligations, and the machinations of goldfish brokers, not a few goldfish lovers drove their families into bankruptcy and drifted into oblivion – all over goldfish. One fish lover built enormous facilities in an attempt to breed the ideal goldfish of his feverish dreams, one that would incorporate all the best features of existing types. He wanted to combine the unadorned countenance and fleshy back of the *wakin* with the fecund breast and belly of the *ryūkin*. The fins should envelop the body as they swayed, like the gown of a goddess; the body should glisten with a myriad of freshly painted colours and, most important, it should be spangled with black dots at coquettish intervals, like the bolero jacket of a Spanish dancer.

This enchanting goldfish of surreal beauty was no mere product of Mr G's imagination. Indeed, as he bred goldfish with goldfish, it came closer and closer to reality. But in the process it was Mr G who lost touch with reality. When he had run through all of his assets, he became a raving idiot and went missing. He was last seen running away dressed like a beggar and calling out the name he had planned to give to the fish he wanted to create: 'Kaguya hime'! The strange, half-completed fish he had bred and the story of his fate were all that remained among his fellow goldfish breeders.

'If Mr G had not lost his mind and had managed to keep a clear enough head to pursue his research scientifically and create the ideal goldfish, I think he would have been a courageous hero.'

Masako went on to praise the path upon which Mataichi was about to enter, saying what an artistic and godlike endeavour it was to unleash a gorgeous ethereal creation into the water, a creation made – unlike painting, sculpture, or architecture – from the stuff of life itself. She continued to encourage Mataichi as they walked, all the way to Reinanzaka, where they stopped at the American Bakery.

Inside, they could hear the soft, plaintive sound of the wings of a couple of moths flocking to the clear light of the chandelier hanging from the vaulted ceiling. As the two sat quietly drinking tea directly beneath the chandelier, Mataichi responded with a question.

'What do you plan to do, Masako? Not that I have any clue myself, but what are you thinking of? You've finished school and become so beautiful…' Suddenly Mataichi felt tongue-tied and could not go on. The white expanse of Masako's face coloured a bit with embarrassment, and she gathered her dangling kimono sleeves.

'Me? I suppose I'm prettier than some, but I'm just a normal woman. In two or three years I'll end up getting married and become a mother like anyone else.'

'Surely marriage is not such a casual matter as that.'

'But you can't go looking all over the world for a partner, and it's not easy to get everything you want in a marriage. We're not as free as all that, after all.'

These were the words of a person who had given up hope. And yet they echoed neither with resentment over the mediocrity of life nor with the curiosity or passion of someone who has bounced back from despair to turn the page to an unknown future.

'Someone with such a passive attitude towards life has no business puffing up an irresolute young man like myself with talk of heroism and courage.'

Mataichi felt an inexplicable anger rise within him. Masako was quietly biting her lip halfway in a rare reversion to childhood habit; but eventually replied, 'I am like that, but when I look at you I feel like encouraging you. It's not my fault. I think there's a feeling inside you, a kind of dissatisfaction that I can sense. And that's what makes me talk to you this way.'

For a while silence reigned between the two. As he sat wordlessly facing Masako, Mataichi felt an incalculable beauty burning itself out of her life, scattered mercilessly into space. As his breast filled with affection for her, Mataichi was seized with the desire to embrace her so firmly that all his inescapable irritation and solicitude might stop the flower petals from scattering. But instead he sighed.

'It sure is a quiet night,' was all he could manage to say.

The experimental fisheries station where Mataichi was enrolled as a researcher was on the shore of a large lake in the Kansai region. O City, the seat of the prefectural government, was just a short after-dinner walk away.

Mataichi rented a small room in the annex of an artisan's shop specialising in making wooden *magemono* and *oribako* boxes. He led the simple life of a student, though with a technical bent, spending his days at the fisheries station and his evenings in town drinking beer and watching movies. There were only ten research students, including those at the advanced level, and they formed a close-knit group. Each of them focused on a highly specialised area of research, be it freshwater fish, fish farming, fish catching, or fish preservation, and most of them had been sent to the fisheries station by a government office, a corporation, or another organisation that had guaranteed them employment upon completion of their studies. The fact that their careers as technicians in the fisheries industry were set seemed to impart to them a naively forthright and choleric temperament. Most of them were from provincial backgrounds. In such a crowd, Mataichi stood out as a clever and discerning young man. The fact that he was specialising in pet goldfish, together with their mistaken interpretation of his urbane sensibilities, made the other students treat him as a breed apart, calling him an artist, a poet, and a genius. For Mataichi it felt quite odd to be referred to in this way since he not only considered himself undeserving of these titles but was also contemptuous of them.

The professor under whom Mataichi was studying made good use of him by sending him out often to fulfil certain of his social obligations and undertake negotiations. As he thus became a regular business visitor to certain families involved in the fisheries industry around the lake, he made the acquaintance of several young women of marriageable age. Enthralled by the atmosphere of the big city, these girls were riveted by Mataichi, who seemed to them an exemplar of the smart urban youth. As for Mataichi, he found the attention quite palpably stimulating. In the bars in town he also enjoyed a far warmer reception from the women than other customers.

And yet, having left Tokyo, Mataichi was surprised to find that the person he felt the strongest bond with was Masako, and that this bond was not the result of any reappraisal of her on his part.

It was something to do with her lack of personality. She was an unstoppable woman who simply blossomed like a beautiful butterfly. She overflowed with charm, and yet her charm was only of a physiological sort. She sometimes said clever things, but one was left with the impression of a mechanical doll that spoke through a special talking apparatus; or of an ineffable, far-off, and eerie creature. There was no other way of perceiving her. In no way did she come across as one of those women whose soul is suffused with the portion of sensuality and the whiff of carnality natural to her sex. She was a woman born without passion. Perhaps because he had thought of her in this way, Mataichi had felt a sense of relief when he left Tokyo. He was saying goodbye to a mannequin doll. Farewell to that inhuman siren. Farewell!

Or so he thought for the first couple of months, when he was still distracted by the novelties of the move and his enrolment in school. But soon his student's life on the lake became as normal as the air he breathed, and between the routine of morning and night he began to feel his heart caught up and wrenched by something intensely bleak, regrettable, and painful. He thought of Masako as a female flower that dies as the last of its species without ever encountering a stamen, as a young girl acting without volition and without realising that she is a marionette being manipulated by some great, unseen power. When he thought of her in this way he was overwhelmed by pity and found it impossible as a man to sit idly by. Then Mataichi's attitude towards life in general became so dispirited that he despaired of ever finding a way to replace Masako's insides with those of a real human being. The resulting blue-cold sense of emptiness dyed the substance of his hot, youthful ambition with a lonely pleasure, and he released a quiet sigh from the depths of his lungs. And yet Mataichi gradually began to feel proud of this mysterious love.

Mataichi's thoughts about goldfish changed completely as well, though it is not clear whether the change was related to this love. Despite their unreal appearance, he began to see in goldfish the shape of life itself. They lazed about as if no one were watching, swallowed infinity like gulps of air, and blithely brought to bear the real meaning of manliness by swimmingly rearranging life's priorities according to their own convenience. Mataichi was struck with astonishment.

He had grown up in a goldfish-raising family from childhood to early manhood, had watched them morning, noon, and night until he was sick of the sight, but they had held no more interest for him than firefly carcasses. Goldfish for Mataichi were just fragile, slovenly creatures covered in red rags, pulled through the scummy pond water with rough holes torn in their bellies by little water bugs. In the seven or eight ponds his family kept, the goldfish were mostly left to their own devices, but each year they grew in number until the surface of the water seemed scattered with autumn leaves. Their struggle for the survival of their species yielded enough extra fish for Mataichi and his parents to eke out a meagre living. And Mataichi thought of those rubbishy goldfish as he did scraps of wood or anything else of a purely practical nature.

Mataichi's adoptive father was a middle-aged man without the skills to raise fancy goldfish. The best he could do was a five- or six-year-old *hibuna*, but otherwise he traded in the cheapest varieties. Since coming to the fisheries station, Mataichi had come to know goldfish that were like works of art. Of course they had *ranchū* and oranda lionheads, but also *deme ranchū* with protruding eyes, *chōtengan*, *shūkin*, *shubunkin*, *zenranshi*, calico, and *azumanishiki*. And they even had a certified American comet goldfish, a breed that first came into existence at the Washington Fisheries Bureau and that American specialists had worked hard to stabilise. This last fish was so active it seemed more like a fighting fish than a goldfish. This rich collection of fish was all placed under Mataichi's care, and each morning they waited for him to come and feed them.

When he changed the water in their tanks, they would relieve themselves with what looked like pleasure of long, rainbowlike droppings that picked up colour from the sunlight.

As his research picked up pace, Mataichi gradually became more reclusive, rarely stirring out except to walk back and forth between his laboratory and his room in the annexe of the shop. But the more of a recluse he became, the more he was flooded with invitations from the young woman by the lake.

This young woman was the daughter of a fishing family with a white-walled storehouse where floating nets were always put out to dry. Her house lay in the shadow of the promontory where the local castle stood, a little more than a mile across the lake. Her name was Yoshie. She had a quick temper and could be quite mischievous, but at the same time she had the strength of a Kansai woman, as tenacious as cotton floss.

The fisheries station had asked her family to hand over any rare fish they caught in the lake, and Mataichi was supposed to go and pick them up, but lately he had completely stopped going to Yoshie's house. Another student came in his place. Of course Yoshie had never thought of Mataichi as a serious lover who would be around for the long term anyway. She just assumed that he was finally turning selfish, like men do, or had found another woman to keep him busy. And yet even as she told herself these things, she couldn't help trying to figure out what he was up to. She got her elder brother, who was secretary of the Fishery Study Group, to invite Mataichi to the town on the cape for a few days to give lectures, and she prodded her brother's children into writing him innocent postcards so that she could infer his mood from the wording of his answers. She was less and less sure of a meaningful reply from him to her own letters and telephone calls. She did housework for her elder brother and his wife, a job she managed with great skill. Rumours had spread all around the lake that she and Mataichi were more involved than they actually were, so she stayed away from the fisheries station.

'This is the second autumn since I left Tokyo.'

Mataichi looked out across the surface of the lake, smooth as a mirror in the evening calm, as he untied the mooring of the motorboat. M Mountain towered mightily, Fuji-like, above the flat sand of the opposite shore, and the evening sun, so gentle you could stare at it without hurting your eyes, hung crisp and heavy in the sky like the copper pull of a sliding screen. He started the boat's motor and slipped out onto the surface of the lake, leaving a long wake like a wagtail's tail, as the calm of the landscape was shattered by the hammering of the pistons.

As Mataichi's boat neared the tip of the beach on the opposite shore where people went to swim, he could see the lake extending in three directions. To his left, the largest expanse of the lake opened like a cul-de-sac, and a barely crimson evening mist made the water's surface appear even larger. On his right he could see fishermen's houses on the high ground that rose above a reed swamp and divided the other entrance to the lake from the source of the S River, which was the only outlet for the lake water. A steel railroad bridge and a wooden bridge for people and horses could both be seen spanning the S River, and when a train crossed the steel bridge puffing smoke, the whole scene took on a toy-like quality.

Mataichi brought the boat close to the beachhead. For the evening, the wind was quite strong there, and the waves were rough like the ocean as the carp jumped wildly. He let the boat drift toward the outlet to the river to avoid the wind, and the castle keep on the promontory peeked out from the shadows of a pine forest. The net-patterned image of Yoshie's village filled his eyes. But, as always, he brought his boat back below the plain separating the lake's entrance and the S River, anchored at his usual spot just outside the reed marsh, and tried to enjoy his evening solitude on the lake.

Mataichi sprawled face up in the boat. Before he knew it, the last warmth of the day had cooled and the pallor of the sky was clear as polished steel. Just as the sky took on this sword-like colour, the curly crimson clouds that had been scattered across it like wood shavings resolved into the white of mica. Lifting his head a little, Mataichi could see a perfectly round moon over O City. By contrast, the rows of city lights glowed dim and red, and the slopes of zigzagging peaks spread southward like the panels of a folding screen, shading steeply into crude folds of inky black.

As the waves grew quiet on the opposite shore, the smooth gurgling sound of water welling up from inside the lake filled Mataichi with a familiar comfort. At this point in the lake, a freshwater spring rose somehow from the bottom, causing a ceaseless whirlpool as water lifted water to the surface and scattered it in all directions. The spot was called 'Moku Moku' by locals in imitation of the sound of the water bubbling up from below. Tea masters from Kyoto sent cars there to fetch water because it was said to be the best in the lake. A couple had once thrown themselves in, hoping to commit love suicide here, but the water had borne them back to the surface and kept them from dying. The place was famous for a number of reasons.

The muddy sand in the area was full of willow trees, and Mataichi had discovered this spot while gathering the willow roots in which his goldfish liked to lay their eggs. 'Goldfish make me feel alive, Masako gives me the pathos of love, and for physical intimacy I have Yoshie. My existence is certainly divided up neatly.' Listening to the sound of the water welling up in the whirlpool, Mataichi's loneliness wrung the focus of his complaint even tighter.

Mataichi lay face up in a dreamlike state, half awake and half asleep. On the blurred plank of his consciousness, the colour of a dry photographic plate, Masako's white face bobbed into view, identifiable only by those enormous smouldering eyes. The fins of goldfish danced disembodied, unfurling their beautiful black spots in midair. And part of Yoshie's flesh showed itself sensuously, like a dish meant to stimulate the appetite. These images jostled for position in Mataichi's mind, fading and re-appearing in turn. At the same time, things and forms with no meaning appeared among them, and idle thoughts intruded unnecessarily. Obsessive ideas came and went busily, sometimes lighting up the interior of Mataichi's mind so brightly that his eyes opened to the sky, leaving his head pleasantly fatigued.

At some point Mataichi's body shifted onto its left side. As the boat leaned with him, he could see the dark blue evening-coloured surface of the lake. On the flat sand beach amidst the evening colour, the white waves seemed to grow larger as night advanced. With a swishing sound devoid of any sense of perspec-tive, they seemed now in front and now behind his waking and sleeping consciousness, placing him in an intermediary world belonging neither to the light nor to the dark. In the end, it was no longer clear whether the hazy, dry photographic plate of his consciousness was the evening-coloured scene, or whether that scene was his consciousness. This lack of clarity persisted, only to deepen and overflow with the pleasant sense that a power was at work here that could make anything happen.

Mataichi's heart, free from all entanglements, began to think in the space between dream and reality. The half-sacred and half-

24

human creatures of Greek myths are not imaginary. They actually exist. They are alive in the world even today. They are tired of reality and have lost their patience with its violence and vulgarity. Their sensitive natures have made them flee it, but they have too great a life-force to die. Yet they are too childlike and attached to everyday life to become gods or heavenly creatures. So they linger in our world and have their fun. The true home of Masako and those dazzling goldfish lies in the other world, and they just poke their heads into the real world from time to time. Otherwise those beautiful faces, somewhere between the real and the ideal, could never remain so serene. Indeed, that wide-eyed, vulnerable expression of someone who has always just got out of bed was surely just a mask for Masako and the goldfish. Behind that mask was a satirical clarity that looked down on reality and critiqued it from a superhuman perspective. Mataichi wanted desperately to see Masako again.

The sound of the waves grew louder, and another boat seemed to be suspended over the surface of the lake, enveloped in a lingering white mist that held the light of the moon shining clearly at the top of the sky. He could hear the sound of oars, so he knew it was not a dream. Then he could see the shape of a woman rowing towards him. She came closer. He saw her raise one hand to pull back loose strands of hair. As she turned her face upward, he examined it in the moonlight. It was Yoshie. Mataichi quickly closed his eyes, as if to avoid something he should not have seen.

The bow of the woman's boat brushed against the side of Mataichi's.

'Oh, are you sleeping?'

'...'

'Are you asleep?'

Having rowed right up to him, the woman held her breath for a moment and gazed at Mataichi's sleeping face.

'A few of our boats came back and said you had gone to Moku Moku in the motorboat alone. So I came after you.'

'That's good. I really wanted to see you.'

Mataichi's sudden warmth struck the woman as sarcasm.

'What kind of sleep talk is that? You can be as rude as you want but I'm not going home. And if you're trying to fool me by pretending to be asleep, I'm telling you I won't have it. I may be just a country fisherman's daughter who can't compare with those refined city girls, but – '

'Idiot! Shut up!'

Mataichi yelled without budging an inch from his position, face up in his boat. His voice rang out harshly over the water and shocked Yoshie.

'I don't like sarcastic women like you. If you came to talk rubbish like that you can get the hell out of here.'

Even with his eyes closed, Mataichi could sense the woman trembling with mortification and jealousy.

Yoshie was suppressing her sobs and swallowing her tears. But she calmed down surprisingly soon, and he could hear the sound of water being ladled up by the side of the boat. Mataichi deliberately shifted his focus, stole a glance at her, then immediately closed his eyes again. She was fixing her tear-streaked face with a hand-mirror in the moonlight. Something hot flew like a dragon at an angle through his heart, but when he thought of Masako, a beautifully vague state of mind enveloped him again like a red mist. Yoshie put her hand on the side of her boat as if she had just remembered something and, replacing her prickly tone with a sickly sweet smile, said softly, 'Can I get in your boat?'

'Yeah…' Suddenly Mataichi was struck by a feeling: everyone is frustrated and sad. You might think you have enough but something is always lacking somewhere. No one can have everything they want. And everyone is lonely. Mataichi was overcome with pity for others and for himself.

Meigetsu ya
Kosui wo wataru
Nana Komachi.

Under the harvest moon
They cross the lake together.
All Seven Komachis.

Was this one of Bashō's poems? I'm not sure, but Mataichi said something like it as his arm stretched out to rest on Yoshie's shoulder. Yoshie allowed herself to be drawn toward him, folding herself like an invertebrate animal into whatever awkward position he liked.

From time to time Mataichi tried sending casual correspondence to Masako. On a postcard with a picture of the lake, he wrote that he washed his shirts in its clean water. On one with a picture of an island, he told her how he had borrowed two *sen* from the inn where he stayed to cover the price of the ferry.

For every three or four of his letters, there was a single reply from Masako. And they were quite impersonal when they did come.

'The other day I asked my poet friend, Miss Fujimura, to come over and we started doing research on the fashions of the baroque period.' Or, 'Miss Fujimura and I went to Nikkō to see the "Sleeping Cat" by Hidari Jingorō, the brilliant sculptor of Japan's baroque period. It was quite adorable.'

It was becoming increasingly apparent that she was drifting free of reality.

Mataichi knew nothing about this baroque period, so he looked it up in an encyclopedia in the fisheries station library. Apparently it referred to a style of the seventeenth century, when the humanism of the European Renaissance drifted away from a focus on nature towards the sublimation of human artistry. It was a time when desperately ornate forms of purely human invention blossomed in profusion like artificial flowers. When he compared this to what he had been studying about the history of goldfish, it occurred to Mataichi that it corresponded to the Genna era (1615–24), when goldfish were first imported and admired in Japan. So goldfish were a product of the baroque period. Was there anything about Masako that did not eventually lead back to goldfish?

Mataichi still felt both pity and contempt for Masako as a woman who resembled an icon out of step with her age. But soon he grew anxious as the desire rose within him to topple her transcendence, to lure her back to reality and forge a blood connection of her carnal desire with his. He had attempted this many times, only to give up in indecision, but each time he felt the desire burn within him, and he was filled with a fresh passion that he could not ignore.

'Physiology and everyday life both demand that we appreciate the flesh of the opposite sex. One of the women on the lake here has been so kind as to offer me hers.'

Mataichi himself thought this an obnoxious thing to say, but there was no helping it. As he wrote to Masako, emphasising that his relations with Yoshie were now fading in intensity, when in fact they had ended after a very short time, he felt that the battle with Masako had begun in earnest. He savoured a solitary rush of excitement. However she might answer the letter, her response would surely betray whatever portion of womanliness she possessed. Testing Masako was now even more urgent than his goldfish research, even if it meant running the risk that her father would find out and cut off his tuition payments.

'This woman is not as beautiful as you are, but...' he wrote, but was unable to continue with 'she's not as icy as you are, either.' Mataichi forced a smile.

With each letter Mataichi upped the ante and goaded himself into describing his relations with Yoshie in more emotional detail, but Masako's replies gave off not a spark of the woman's body he wanted to discover there. Instead she just wrote about goldfish: how she and her father were growing more and more fascinated by them, and that while her father's interest had to do with profit, her own sprang from a strangely selfless appreciation and affection. As long as he did not neglect his goldfish research, she seemed to be saying, she could not care less what woman he was seeing. Just when Mataichi was nearing exhaustion from her constant evasion of his feelings for her, he received the following letter.

'I'm sorry to have kept silent while you confessed so much. I'm having a baby soon. And then I'm going to get married. I know the order is backwards. But it's not that passionate an affair anyway.'

Mataichi didn't know how to react. This was a woman born to walk lightly through the air right above the path that the rest of us tread.

'The other party is none of the three young men you know. He is a bit more forthright and not the sort of man to be unkind or do anyone harm. For me that is more than enough.'

Mataichi looked back and saw the futility of all his fussing and cleverness. The surprising realisation that even in the present age a woman could live so boldly, like a straight thick line, gave Mataichi the sense of a kind of modernity in Masako.

'It's none of my business, but I think you should marry that lady. I find getting married makes you want others to do it too. But work hard on your goldfish. You've got to come up with a new breed, a fabulous one so beautiful that it makes you forget everything when you look at it. It's strange, but I'm more excited to see the goldfish born from your research than the baby I'm about to have. You know, I've convinced father to put even more effort into our goldfish venture.'

Teizō's letter arrived at around the same time. In it he gave an honest account of his family's financial situation since the crisis. It had not been easy, but resolute cutbacks had made it possible for him to preserve a small but solid base and he planned to pour all of his resources into the breeding and sales of goldfish, where the export prospects were one hundred percent. He wanted Mataichi to stop thinking of himself as a scholarship student with leisure and to start working as a technician in the business and devote himself to this enterprise. In exchange, he would increase the money he was sending to the level of a proper salary.

Instead of feeling relieved that his career was made, Mataichi resisted angrily. He chafed at the idea that the bastards from the mansion on the hill, father and daughter alike, were trying to swallow him whole.

Mataichi did not reply to Masako or her father. Instead, he completely abandoned his goldfish research and stumbled in a daze into the nightlife of Kyoto. But after a month he came back with his mind already made up. He would create a precious, beautiful new breed of goldfish like none the world had ever seen. Making this his life's work, he would think of himself as a man blessed with a tragic form of happiness shared by no other, as a nameless hero caught up in a mysterious fate. He was determined to succeed even if it cost him his life. Would this mean he was being taken advantage of by the father and daughter from the house on the hill? If so, then so be it. If it meant making Masako happy as he had always wanted, this happiness would link the two of them together... and yet how strange and sad it was that this unreal beauty should be snared by the unreal beauty of a fish. From the window of his laboratory he looked out onto the lake, as syrupy as liquid candy. Gazing at it, he flicked his tongue to the back of his throat, trying to wipe clean the memory of cherry petals that still seemed stuck from when Masako had thrown them at him as a child.

'Masako. Masako.' As he called her name, he let go tears so sentimental even he thought it strange. Rumours started to circulate that Mataichi's nerves were frazzled and that he was on the verge of a breakdown. In fact, there was something quite frightening about his appearance as he stood alone late at night in the dark laboratory, preparing specimens. In the hushed darkness of the laboratory, Mataichi sat with only a single lamp lit on his table and sliced open one goldfish after another, cutting lengthwise and crosswise to carve out their organs and scatter them over the tabletop. As he peered into his microscope at these organs, nudging them around with tweezers deep into the night with a concentration so complete he forgot the hour, Mataichi resembled a nocturnal beast who, having stumbled across a surprisingly large cache of food, had momentarily forgotten to eat it and was playing with it instead. The severed heads of goldfish stared with eyes shining like rubies in the light of the electric lamp. They opened and closed their mouths from time to time as if they had just remembered something.

For a young man raised in the city and accustomed to wide-ranging intellectual stimulation, it was twice as difficult for Mataichi as it would have been for most people to narrow the focus of his talent to the genetics and reproduction of goldfish, a field that not only constituted a specialty within a specialty but also demanded patience and a tolerance for monotony. When his cheeks and eyes had hollowed and he felt sapped of all his strength, Mataichi would slouch over to the edge of the window and place his hand on the cover of one of the glass jars arrayed there. The blood ran cold in his icy fingertips, but accumulated excitement sent a charged current through them and made them tremble and entwine together. When he finally opened the cover, the calicos, prized among goldfish, lay sleeping with their eyes open above a small rock. Awakening to the light of the electric lamp, the pair that had been lying together began to swim at a leisurely pace, now in tandem and now apart. Their tail fins were three or four times larger than their bodies were wide or long, so when they unfurled their delicate silk fins and gowns spangled with black stars, their bodies and heads were momentarily obscured. But soon there bobbed into view, like a corpulent French beauty or a graceful and majestic woman of the Tempyō era, a round body, eyes, and a mouth with eyebrows that made you want to paint them.

These goldfish had been awarded the gold medal at a fisheries fair in O City a few years earlier. They were subsequently donated to the fisheries station and were kept there with great care. They were already seven or eight years old, which made them just beyond middle age and gave them a calm and refined charm.

After gazing at them for a while, Mataichi replaced the lid on the jar and went back to his seat, where he contorted his body repeatedly in the same manner as the goldfish. When people asked him about this, he would laugh, saying it was his 'goldfish exercise', and proceed to tout its health benefits. But as he performed the exercise this time, he felt a more secret, constitutive power return to his spirit and his body. This Mataichi kept to himself.

In any case, it was really spooky to see someone twisting around like a fish in the middle of the night. Or so the night watchman said. 'Would you at least stop that when I come into the room? It gives me the willies.'

Mataichi set out to visit locations in Nara and Osaka prefectures that were famous in the Kansai area for breeding goldfish. Kōriyama City in Nara Prefecture has a particularly long tradition of goldfish breeding, going back to the time when the local lord made raising goldfish the exclusive right of domain samurai as a means of supplementing their otherwise insufficient incomes.

Mataichi stayed for a time in this charming little city that was surrounded by fields of rape blossoms, and acquired a lot of information useful for his work. But he was particularly struck by the discovery of indications in the historical records that local breeders had already come up with a new variety of goldfish in the Hōei era (1704–11), and that from then on they had continued to produce excellent new breeds quite often. The ideal beauty that human beings seem to have sought in goldfish at the time was mostly realised in the famous goldfish brought to perfection in the current Taishō period. And yet the fact that the goldfish of his time still had to live up to that ideal made Mataichi realise just how extravagant a beauty those people of long ago had sought in these fish. The world changes as generation follows generation. And yet the goldfish, a creature meant not to be eaten but only appreciated for its beauty, had somehow managed to approach the goal of self-perfection, overcoming any number of vicissitudes thanks only to the feeble power of beauty. It seemed that it was not human beings who made goldfish, but that the goldfish themselves had continued doggedly towards their goal by seducing and exploiting the weakest of human instincts – the one driven by beauty. Goldfish were a force to be reckoned with! This insight into their strength supplemented Mataichi's goldfish obsession with something like a conqueror's lust.

That summer he completed his field study, and after he had settled back into his lodgings by the lake for a couple of weeks, the news reached him of the Great Kantō Earthquake. At first he thought little of it. But gradually he began to realise how terrible it had been. The Yamanote region had been spared, it seemed, but soon there were reports of horrific devastation in other parts of Tokyo. Mataichi cabled home to ask if he should return to Tokyo. Ten days later his mind was finally put at ease by the reply, which read 'Not necessary.'

Soon after, Teizō began contacting Mataichi quite often with business requests and inquiries regarding the goldfish.

When he wrote to Teizō, worried that people would have lost interest in something as frivolous as goldfish in the wake of such a disaster, Teizō replied, 'The old people tell me that since the time of the shogunate goldfish have always sold very well after disasters like this. Goldfish are the only things that can make people feel better as they huddle in temporary shelters amid burnt-out ruins. The goldfish industry in Tokyo has resolved to hold its ground and rebuild to twice its former scale.'

At first Mataichi was rather sceptical and took Teizō's letter as the kind of hyperbole practised so skilfully by business types, but he was mistaken. Goldfish sent to the market at a twenty percent increase quickly rose another twenty percent, and still supply could not keep up with demand.

The goldfish farms in Tokyo's Shitamachi had all been destroyed, but those in the Yamanote area survived. It was also possible to import goldfish from the Kansai region, so that numbers were not lacking, but the loss to fire of many goldfish barrels was a great blow. Dealers shared the ones they had on hand and sent people all over to order new ones.

What with managing these imports, ordering new barrels, and other business to attend to, Mataichi would have to stay in Kansai for some time yet.

Eventually Teizō called Mataichi back to Tokyo, where he returned after an absence of four years. In the end, his thesis went unfinished. Six months earlier, in the fall, his classmates whose research was simpler than Mataichi's had submitted their theses, received their diplomas, and set off to take up the posts promised them. Mataichi asked Teizō to delay his return to Tokyo so that he could finish his thesis. And he could have done so had he set his mind to it, but the truth was he had nothing but contempt for such a tidy little achievement, one that had no connection to how he was feeling. He was impatient to get back to his own ponds and create with his own hands even one dazzling goldfish that would resemble Masako. And having created it, he yearned to sing a song of victory. This was the only hope left in his life now.

In the beginning, he was resolved to create a goldfish of unprecedented beauty in order to give Masako what she wanted. But with the passage of time and the progress of his research, his mind had changed as well. If he was finally unable to have the real Masako for himself, he wanted to create a beautiful goldfish that would remind him of her as a kind of compensation. And this desire eventually conquered his initial resolve.

Masako's ethereal beauty. Only the opulent beauty of the goldfish could even begin to suggest it. Now Mataichi's success in his research was becoming more and more a desperate matter for his very existence. Realising this, Mataichi lay exhausted on his bed at night, unable to close his eyes as they blazed out in the darkness.

'What an idiot you are! If you could just put your work together into a thesis, it would be useful for goldfish researchers all over the world.'

Mataichi had said his goodbyes to the disgruntled professor who still had high hopes for him, and returned to Tokyo as a dropout. The thought occurred to him of burning his unfinished manuscript or throwing it into the lake, but he could not even muster such a theatrical gesture. Feeling only that it was slightly more valuable than a pile of trash, he stuffed it into his bag and came home.

It was the spring of the year following the earthquake, so the Shitamachi district was still in terrible shape, but the Yamanote area was as it had always been. At the house in the ravine the position of the water source had shifted a little so the ponds were supplied with water by means of bamboo pipes bandaged with rope made from hemp palm.

Mataichi climbed up to the big house on the cliff to announce that he had returned home and to report for work.

After thanking him for his efforts in shipping goldfish from Kansai, Teizō said to Mataichi, 'You know, I've actually got a little carried away and started raising carp and eel as well, but I'm relying on other people to do it for me and it's not going very well. They're all freshwater fish so they can't be that different from goldfish. What do you think about taking care of them for me? Since they're edible, we'll have a much bigger market if we succeed.'

Mataichi, of course, promptly refused.

'I'm afraid I can't. That's like asking someone who writes poems to plough a field. Besides, I want you to let me focus on breeding the highest-quality goldfish. If you allow me to do this, I will work as if my life depended on it. I don't need a wife, and I don't care about prolonging my family line. All I want out of life is to create gorgeous new breeds of goldfish. I'm sorry if this makes you feel that your money has gone for a purpose other than what you anticipated.'

Seeing Mataichi's enthusiasm, Teizō knew there was no use arguing and immediately started to figure out a way to turn this obsession into something useful to his business.

'Sounds interesting. Go ahead then. Take your time until you get the results you're looking for.'

Teizō seemed to get a thrill out of his own magnanimous words and, feeling a bit heroic for the first time in a while, said he wished he could sit down to dinner with Mataichi but that he

36

had a previous engagement he could not get out of. Instead, he sent the maid to get Masako and her husband to stand in for him and left.

Mataichi had a few moments of bated breath until the door to the parlour opened halfway and Masako, sporting a surprisingly bashful expression, angled her upper body into view.

'It's been a while.'

She seemed reluctant to come in. Mataichi felt a gentle sigh escape him of its own accord, the sigh of someone for whom the mere sight of a longed-for object is enough to quench his thirst. He wanted to laugh and smile with her unconditionally, even as the sadness of his lonely state welled up within him, but something stopped him. He was made wary by a suspicion that doing so would leave him to be trampled upon by her charms and easily robbed of the determination he had so carefully maintained. So, instead, his pride took advantage of the unexpected weakness she had displayed, and he summoned his courage in order to appear as strong and gruff as possible. Putting on the authoritative air of an elderly man who has seen many hardships, he said, 'Well, come in then. Why are you just standing there?'

Like a child, she hid her face behind the door, then opened it properly. As she came into the room, Mataichi noted that her breasts were as firm as before and her head sat pertly above her shoulders. Her expression was as distant as ever – the lips curved in a half-smile as sweet as honey and her large, slightly downcast eyes smouldered like pointed swords. Her eyebrows were drawn in thickly, as was the fashion. Mataichi kept looking at the floor and, feeling that he had lost a battle of wills, crawled sadly back into his lonely shell.

'It's been a while. You've lost a lot of weight, haven't you?'

But she had not looked him over as carefully as this might suggest. 'Yes. I've had a hard time of it.'

'Really? They say hardship is good medicine.'

For a while their conversation turned to the earthquake and to the lake where Mataichi had been living.

'Have you come up with a good goldfish?'

For a number of reasons Mataichi found it difficult to answer this question. He plucked up his courage and struck back.

'And how's your husband?'

'Oh, he's fine.'

She glanced out the window at the thick stand of trees alongside the main house.

'He's not here now. He likes basketball, you know, and he's gone to the YMCA. Won't be back until just before dinner. Ha-ha-ha.'

It was extremely painful for Mataichi to deduce from her way of speaking that she was not without love for her husband, whom she seemed to treat like a child. He found it impossible to continue and ask her about her children.

'I could introduce you, but I don't think you would find him very interesting.'

That was for sure. Masako was Mataichi's idol, and he had to be content that her husband was not the type to break her spirit. In fact, he could feel more at ease as long as she was with an unremarkable man.

'Thanks for sending me presents sometimes.'

'This is a piece of porcelain made by the lake.' Mataichi put down a package wrapped in paper and stood up.

'Oh, you shouldn't have. But it is so nice to have you back, Mataichi.'

Mataichi felt a bit let down by how mediocre she seemed in person. He wondered how it could be that his whole life had been under the sway of a woman like this. As he headed back down the cliff in the early evening gloom, the bush warblers were singing and yellow rose petals were scattering in the breeze. Once again Mataichi recalled the cherry petals Masako had showered him with as a child and unconsciously probed the back of his throat with his tongue. There was no question about it: he was in love with her. But his love had wandered off course and was dangling free in midair. It was too late to confront her with it outright, but neither could he keep it pent up inside. So all he could do was use the goldfish, those creatures to which he was so accustomed, to create one of her for himself. Mataichi looked down at the ponds in the valley far below him and mustered an extravagant courage.

Mataichi was not displeased when they finished building a modest laboratory out of concrete and a new-style breeding pool in the garden of the house in the ravine. He sequestered himself there with a single-minded resolve and cut off all contact with friends and relatives. He also intimated to the people in the mansion on the cliff that they should stay away until his research was complete.

'Bury yourself beneath the surface and enter the marrow of life.' Such a sentiment was not without substance for Mataichi. To create one's lover with one's own hands… A star born beautiful and new to the world… No one anywhere knows what it feels like. Mataichi lost himself in sad and straitened emotions. In an antique shop in Kōriyama he had found a drawing titled 'Sacred Fish with Corydalis'. He had it framed and hung it on the wall, and now he gazed at it from a chair he put out on the veranda for the purpose.

The early summer breeze blew gently across him. The volatile smell of green leaves was in the air. Suddenly he began to worry whether the middle-aged calico goldfish were being properly taken care of back at the fisheries station.

'If I'm too much of a coward to let old things like those die, I'll never be up to the task of creating something new.'

At this, Yoshie's figure flitted across his mind.

He forced himself to imagine the calicos suffering from some putrescent disease, their bodies the colour of rust, floating foul-smelling on the surface of the water and unable even to gasp for breath. Then he imagined Yoshie in the same way. A hot current ran up both sides of his spine and pushed oppressively at the base of his throat. He bit his lip and stuck out his jaw.

'I'm fine,' he said.

It was already too late in the year for goldfish breeding, and scum was still covering the ponds. So Mataichi gave up on getting them to lay eggs and instead went in search of new fish to breed with. He visited every goldfish breeder in Tokyo, both professionals and amateurs. When they refused to part with a fish he wanted, Mataichi would say awful, venomous things about their fish.

'Mataichi is the worst sort of man. He's like a giant water-bug.'

Soon, this is what everyone in the Tokyo goldfish business thought of Mataichi. The giant water-bug was a ferocious pest that attacked goldfish. But Mataichi did not let their talk bother him, and one way or another he managed to acquire at least one of the female siblings of the fish he wanted. His plan was to produce an ideal goldfish by mating a perfected cultured fish like a calico or a *shūkin* with a different breed.

When the flowering season arrived in the following year, the breeding stars along the males' pectoral fins opened their moistened eyes like the evening sky in spring, thus announcing the beginning of the mating season. Once it began, the fish lost themselves to the power of sex. With very un-fishlike gravitas, they cruised through the water resembling fleets of destroyers and pecked at one another with the lightning precision of fighting cocks. They twisted, flipped, and turned bizarrely in the water in an effort to wash away the slimy mess that burned in their bodies. Mataichi was like a wooden man whose carnal desire had flowed against his will and was channelled almost entirely towards goldfish, but as he watched he was reminded ever so slightly of the allure of the world and soon found himself wandering alone at night in the bar district of Roppongi, or asking for a bottle of beer with his dinner.

It was his adoptive mother, Otsune, who brought it to him, along with the obligatory comment on his marital status.

'Now that we've retired, I sure wish you'd hurry up and find yourself a wife so we can really take it easy.'

'I'm married to my goldfish,' said Mataichi, hiding behind his drunkenness to drive a wedge between himself and this mundane matter. But his mother shot back, 'Well, who knew? As far as I can remember, you never liked goldfish much when you were a kid.'

Encouraged by the recent revival of interest in traditional culture, Sōjūrō, his adoptive father, evinced a desire to go back to teaching *ogiebushi* singing. Reminiscing that it had been forty years since he'd last played, he picked up the shamisen plectrum and sang:

Ogiebushi
Waiting ain't easy.
We're all silent pines rooted in the rock.
This young pine has her secrets too.
When so many other trees have flowers.
The plum, the peach, the cherry – all decked out in blossoms.

Mataichi could not say if he was any good or not. But the gentle sound of the raspy voice heard through the weeping forsythia that stood between him and the main house filled him with pity for this person punting his way precariously along in the stream of attachment.

41

His adoptive father had always turned out ordinary goldfish like so much hay, and since Teizō's company took them off his hands, he never had to bother with sales.

'He buys them so cheap, and an amateur like me is no match for him. But he's taken quite a shine to you, Mataichi. Why don't you pressure him for more?'

Sōjūrō let slip this complaint and disappeared. Later he was walking around pleased as punch, having obtained a significant amount of research money out of Teizō on Mataichi's behalf.

Mataichi paid no attention to any of this and diligently changed the water in the pools. He quietly brought the male and female fish together from the pools in which they had been separated. Then he used a rope and carefully lowered into the pool the now-disinfected willow roots he had brought all the way from the Moku Moku spot on the lake.

The sky was a deep blue that morning, and the sunlight stuck like malt syrup to the wings and the backs of the birds. Mataichi stood on the veranda and put first his hand and then his face out to test the air.

'There's no wind. We're set.'

Pulling back a third of the reeds from the screen intended to shield the pond from the sun, Mataichi fashioned a peephole and waited. Soon three males were advancing in a line like a naval battle charge, trying to chase a single female into the tangle of the willow root. The female was doing her best to avoid them and escape. One wonders why. Was it a virgin's shame? Do all living things treasure their sexual independence? Or was she just a coquette playing hard to get? In the end, she could not escape without scattering her eggs like so many pretty pearls among the tendrils of the willow root. The males' bellies shone with victory as they blitzed each egg in its turn.

42

Suddenly Mataichi realised he was squatting with both elbows on his knees, his hands clasped tightly together, biting his fingers hard and praying with all his might. No matter how insignificant the creature, bringing life into this world is not something to be taken lightly. For a misanthropist like Mataichi, the further the creature giving birth was from human beings the greater the psychological impact. And all the more so now that these goldfish were overcoming their apprehensions about belonging to different breeds to create new life in the service of Mataichi's egoistic goals. He felt infinitely grateful to them.

He gave the fish a break and separated the males from the females. As he boiled a light white-fleshed fish to feed them, Mataichi felt his frail body swell – man that he was – with maternal affection.

But the fry that hatched that year were more showy than even he had hoped and he found them vulgar.

After failing in this way for two successive years, Mataichi began to rethink his strategy from the ground up. He realised that he had been mistaken in his choice of the parent fish that was to provide the bone structure. The fish he wanted had to have the winsome torso of a young girl onto which could be added more elaborate and alluring features. And the only way to get a fish with such a torso was to start with a pure-bred *ranchū*. The winsome, *ranchū*-like figure of Masako as a girl appeared in Mataichi's mind's eye. For the first time in quite a while he felt the same old mortification at the thought of the hold Masako had on him. This time, however, the pain of it was like an old friend.

Mataichi's spirits picked up. He may have surrendered to Masako's influence and gone back to the artlessness of the *ranchū*, but once he had fashioned a fish as beautiful as she was, he could make it the parent of more; and as its offspring gave birth to further generations, no matter how long it took, every step toward beauty would be another victory for him. Telling himself that these beautiful victory fish would be his vassals, Mataichi girded himself for battle. Mataichi knew that he had to be patient for a while. He ordered a splendid parent *ranchū* shipped from Kansai and sat back to wait for the spring breeding season. The torso of the *ranchū* was childlike and adorable, but its face was as fierce as a bulldog. The first task was to cross it with a goldfish with beautiful features to eliminate that fierceness.

Mataichi hardly went near the house on the cliff, so he rarely met Masako's husband, a handsome young gentleman with nervously upturned eyes, a straight nose, and rather pronounced cheekbones, whose body seemed to pulse with sharp masculine electricity. One Sunday morning, he brought Masako and their daughter to the Romanesque tea house and sat reading a foreign newspaper. Just below them, on the pathway up the cliff, Mataichi had collected some worms from a puddle of dirty water to feed his goldfish and was on his way down when he looked up. He acted as if he had not seen them and continued nonchalantly on his way. Masako, who had seen all this, felt a pang of guilt that the two of them were there together, even though he was her husband.

'What are you worried about? And why?' her husband said brusquely.

'Sitting here next to each other like this, we can be seen from anywhere, isn't that right?' Masako pressed the matter calmly.

'What's wrong with people seeing you and me here together?' The husband's words betrayed a hint of annoyance.

'Nothing at all, but the people in the house down there can see us too, you know. And that man is still single.'

'You mean Mataichi, the goldfish expert?'

'Yes.'

At this, her husband showed some agitation, and he said contemptuously,

'I suppose you wish you'd married him instead?'

But Masako stepped outside of his sights and put that distant look on her face.

'You know I'm a stickler for good looks. Certainly in a husband. I couldn't even enjoy a meal with a man who wasn't handsome.'

'You're quite something, you are,' said the husband, unable to get angry or to laugh.

'So! Shall we have a bath?' he said, as he scooped up their daughter and went inside.

What Masako was thinking after that as she sat in the Romanesque tea pavilion was beyond the ability of any normal person to fathom. She seemed to sit there forever, that unreadable gaze smouldering on the linen tablecloth as it caught the lonely winter sun.

'The carp and eel farming isn't going well, and they say Teizō's having a hard time of it. When a fish farm starts eating money, it's no laughing matter.'

No matter how many times he rebuilt the holding wall around his ponds, water from the spring kept washing it away. Teizō had rather carelessly chosen a spot beneath a cliff on the sandy coast of an inlet with half fresh and half salt water. Not only that, but the fish farms in Shizuoka Prefecture were expanding and taking advantage of their proximity to the city to deliver their carp and eel. All of this meant that Teizō's company had a hard battle to sell the fish they raised. But the hardest blow came from the unprecedented crisis that hit the financial world that spring, resulting in a banking moratorium from the end of the cherry blossom season. The bank financing

Teizō shut its doors and the rumour was that it was unlikely to reopen.

'"Do you think you can get Mataichi to cut his research expenses down to a third?" he says to me. You could see the blush even on that dark face of his.'

Sōjūrō agreed to cut Mataichi's research budget to a third, but he still related the story of Teizō's straitened circumstances with relish.

Mataichi listened as if it were someone else's business while he got a pair of *ranchū* just arrived from Kansai ready for the winter. In the pool that he planned to wrap with thick straw matting, the fish busily moved their short tails and fins in the weak winter sunlight, and a warm golden light struck his eyes as it bounced off their grey skins. The fish moved slowly along, their bodies so round and fat as to be ugly and adorable at the same time. Mataichi felt a source of life in the object of his obsession, and a vast expanse of ashes within himself. This made him feel as though split in two and struck him as funny. For the first time in a long time Mataichi laughed out loud. Sōjūrō slapped him on the back and said, 'Don't scare me like that! You're laughing like a maniac. You know not much bothers me, but you're making me nervous.'

Towards the end of the year, Mataichi heard that Masako had given birth to her second daughter, and the New Year passed without a single sighting of her in the chapel on top of the cliff. He first glimpsed her again as the plum trees were coming into bloom. Having given birth a second time, her beauty had become clear as crystal and more spectacular than ever, like the colour of water plants after the water has been changed. Mataichi thought she had even begun to resemble the drawing of the sacred fish with corydalis flowers that he had framed and hung in his laboratory.

Today Masako and her poet friend, Miss Fujimura, had been in the Romanesque gazebo since the afternoon. The two women were having a lively conversation. Even Mataichi, who had grown as aloof from the world as a bag of old bones, wanted to know what they were talking about. Towards evening he pretended that he was going to collect worms, crept quietly to the puddles of dirty water halfway up the cliff and hunkered down. He was not yet thirty, but his body and mannerisms were those of someone already ravaged by age. The two women seemed to have been discussing a topic for some time below, but Mataichi could not hear them clearly from where he was. In fact, the conversation between Miss Fujimura and Masako went something like this: when Masako proposed redecorating her room in rococo style, Miss Fujimura, after what seemed a painful pause, said, 'Four or five years ago, when you were into the baroque style, I already thought it was too artificial, but I kept it to myself. But rococo is even more artificial. It's an aesthetic just one step away from total decadence.'

'But I'm just dying to do it.'

'You're a strange one, Masako.'

'Do you think so? I think I'm just like you said once, the kind of person who looks at the blue sky and clouds and thinks of it as the ocean dotted with islands.'

Mataichi came quietly back down to his garden, walked unobtrusively along the eaves, and entered his laboratory in the gathering dusk. He leaned against its crude chair and closed his eyes tightly. He hardly ever met Masako in person anymore. When, like today, she came with a friend to the chapel, or with her children or her husband, he was usually unable to hear what they were saying. But even from far away Mataichi could feel her presence these days. Perhaps she had forgotten about the matter of the goldfish that she had entrusted to him;

Masako was vaporising into an increasingly unreal beauty, and he felt a delicate sorrow come bubbling up within him.

Having started from the ground up with the *ranchū*, it took Mataichi three years to come up with a fish that had the bone structure he wanted. And then he proceeded to fail year after year.

'The day is short but the road is long.'

Or so said Mataichi when his goldfish did not turn out right. But he only mouthed the words, without investing any emotion. He felt himself turning into a bag of white bones even as he lived and, telling himself that this would not do, he tried to bolster his will by gazing at Masako, even at a distance, and summoning up every drop of hostility, jealousy, and hatred he could muster.

Quite a number of failed, almost-famous goldfish had accumulated in the old pond. Mataichi refused to sell them, so Sōjūrō and his wife tossed food into the old pond beneath the cliff, complaining all the while. They grimaced and said it was like an *obasuteyama* for goldfish.

Ten years of failure passed. There were a few changes both above and below the cliff. Teizō died, and his son-in-law became the master of the mansion on the cliff. He followed in Teizō's footsteps by scaling back their business drastically. Rumour had it that now that Masako's husband had become head of the household, he had become involved with a maid with a face like a Pekinese, whom he treated like a mistress, despite having such a beautiful wife. When the son-in-law took over, the research money from the top of the cliff was cut off and Mataichi became an entirely independent researcher.

Sōjūrō died, and the sign by the road advertising him as an *ogiebushi* instructor came down, although he had only one or two pupils anyway.

Masako still showed herself from time to time in the Romanesque gazebo. These changes in the real world served only to increase the charm of a new tendency to knit her brows. She had the utter serenity of a beauty on the brink of middle age.

In the late autumn of 1932, Tokyo and Yokohama were hit with torrential rains that brought the equivalent of thirty-seven gallons of rainwater for every square yard of land in Tokyo. The ditch in the ravine overflowed, and the half-completed seed fish that Mataichi had so painstakingly crafted were washed away.

In the middle of the autumn of 1935, another storm dropped sixteen gallons of rain per square yard, and almost everything was washed away again.

From then on Mataichi was a nervous wreck each year when autumn came. The slightest low-pressure front would set his nerves on edge, and he would lie awake and trembling throughout the night. He had been suffering from insomnia for some time and had trouble sleeping without medication. But now, as each night brought him closer to autumn, he had to increase his dosage.

That evening, the forecast said nothing about low pressure, but the pitter-patter of rain started late at night. 'This is it,' Mataichi thought. He lay in bed trembling and tried to get up several times, but his mind was cloudy and his body seemed utterly exhausted. As the sound of the rain grew louder, his nerves grew taut, but the strong medication soothed them again and he returned to an even deeper sleep. Mataichi lay face up in bed with his legs poised to get up, his eyes and mouth half open as he snored. It was close to dawn by the time the medicine had worn off enough for him to wake.

The rain had stopped by then, and clouds were racing across the leaden world of the ravine, the trees gathered in their heavy branches like wet umbrellas, dribbling white droplets in disarray. The face of the cliff was black with moisture and layers of sand from which water came oozing out. The Romanesque gazebo on the edge of the cliff receded from view like an ancient fortress, alone and out of step with the rest of the scene in its hardness.

Seven or eight goldfish were motionless among the water plants and thick reeds, which had been trampled by the wind's rampage. The only sound was that of water dripping, and otherwise nothing seemed amiss. The crass cry of a crow tore through the early morning mist above the houses along the road.

The water was high in the ditch, but it had not overflowed and its usual boisterous bubbling was replaced by the steady flow of a now-brimming stream that seemed rather anti-climactic.

'This isn't so bad,' Mataichi mumbled to himself as he went to check the pools just in case, teetering down the red clay path with the hem of his pyjamas sticking to the heels of his bare feet.

When the pools came into view, Mataichi shuddered with horror and felt his heart convulse with shock.

A silent, flat stream of water was leaking from the ditch across an earthen section of the path. It had overturned the reed covers of the pools and opened a gaping hole in the wire netting. As the current flowed into the pools, it hit the bottom and sprang back to the surface to spill over the edges in all directions, like a natural spring.

Peering into the pools, Mataichi could clearly make out the pebbles and shredded water plants on the bottom, but there was no trace of the goldfish.

In a sudden rage, Mataichi kicked away the last remaining portion of the barrier of wire netting, but the force of his kick caused him to slip on his bare feet and he fell over into the current that was running like a waterfall down the clay path. Skin and bones that he was, Mataichi was swept up and carried all the way to the edge of the old pond at the base of the cliff, where he barely managed to stop himself by digging his feet into a mass of rotten leaves and mud.

He had long faced the bleak prospect of many more years of crossbreeding and modifications before he could achieve his ideal new variant, but if he had lost all of his breeder goldfish to this water, it meant that fourteen years of struggle had burst like a bubble and he had lost everything. Mataichi was sapped of all his strength and spirit and lost consciousness for a while, his body crumpled in a heap next to the old pond, dark and deep as a cave.

As Mataichi began to regain consciousness, a rose-coloured dawn was breaking and all things in the ravine pulsed with life. As he watched, the thin clouds above peeled away to reveal a sparkling blue sky, like a sheet of paper just made.

How fresh and forgiving was the breath of the trees and the grasses. Green, madder, orange, and yellow, each and every cluster of leaves swelled and seemed to gasp with a surfeit of life. The dishevelled grasses lightly shook off beads of dew and rearranged themselves luxuriantly like bosoms standing to attention.

Wherever Mataichi bent his ear to listen, there was the babbling sound of water, and the echo of this hastily improvised mountain stream gave a pulse of movement to the landscape before his eyes. Listening with rapt attention, Mataichi felt himself transported along with the very ground beneath him to a boundless space where he might journey forever above the white clouds.

As the varied shadows resolved into a deep azure and the patches of light were gathered up into a single dreamy amber, a corner of the tiled roof beside the road glowed incandescent, releasing violet and white streams of light that splintered again into gleaming streamers spreading over all that faced them in the valley.

The early autumn sun rose like a freshly polished mirror. The cries of birds embroidered lively trails here and there across the fresh tapestry of space.

Having once fainted from shock and then recovered, Mataichi had entered a clear-headed trance. He remembered nothing and thought of nothing, but beheld the beauty of nature as it was, transforming into ecstasy itself.

The warped green outlines of his seven goldfish ponds seemed like the footprints of some primeval beast, and Mataichi stared transfixed at these beautiful spots on the earth. As the sun shone in and his mind cleared, the old pond directly in front of him began to seem like an ancient cave he was seeing for the first time. It was here that Mataichi had left the defective fish he had bred over more than a decade. He could not bring himself to sell them or to let them go, and instead had left them to fend for themselves in this old pond. Sōjūrō and his wife had taken pity on them and fed them from time to time, but after the old couple died there was no one to look after them, and the hapless fish had survived on the water plants and scum in the pond. Mataichi almost never came near the pond because the sight of these strange, botched goldfish was like a record of his failures. The pond was half-covered in straw matting, and sometimes he thought he felt there the lingering presence of melancholy beings full of resentment at having been deprived of their chance at life. But Mataichi told himself this was just a delusion brought on by his weak nerves.

Now the old straw matting had been ripped off by the wind, and the morning sun gave Mataichi his first clear view of the surface of the pond in years. No sooner had he looked than he fixed his gaze on the pond's surface and took a deep breath, as if to head off the onset of some strong emotion. The water was thick with pond scum. And in the centre swayed several dozen billowing folds finer than white gossamer, ravelling and unravelling in calm profusion. They drifted apart and opened again. They were about the size of a white peony flower, which people say fits just inside the circle formed by the thumbs and index fingers of both hands. It was a single goldfish. The gossamer fins shimmered like a kaleidoscope, as bits of violet, scarlet, lilac, and pale blue mixed with spots the colour of ink and old coins. It was spectacular yet tasteful, elegant and artless at once, its movements so mysterious as it swayed and billowed back and forth that it seemed to be manipulated from an infinite distance away. Mataichi's breast swelled, and he wanted to rub his flesh against a tree root or the edge of a rock. His tattered desire, suspended between the real and the unreal, could scarcely stand the shock.

'This is my ideal, the ultimate fish that I spent more than ten years struggling in vain to create. Which of the fish that I tossed into this pond for their defects mated to hatch this? When did it happen, and how?'

As he went over and over this in his mind, Mataichi's desire was gradually overcome, sucked out of him and scattered by sheer fascination. Finally he was rendered immobile by a streak of satisfaction that shot through to the very depths of his heart.

How strange life was. Sometimes what you're looking for is not to be found when you consciously look for it, but suddenly comes to you from an abandoned past or a path you did not expect to take. As this thought flashed through Mataichi's mind, the beautiful fish came back to the surface after a dive and unfurled its billowing fins and tail. Then it turned to face Mataichi head-on, fixing him with its wide eyes, which harboured stars, and its perfectly round mouth.

'Ah! It doesn't look like Masako. And it doesn't look like that drawing of the sacred fish. It's more... it's more... more beautiful than that. It's a goldfish.'

Whether from despair or from a happiness greater than despair, Mataichi's emotion-filled body slid weakly into the mud beside the pond. He remained there, his eyes tightly shut and his shoulders rising rhythmically as he breathed. Meanwhile, just beneath the surface of the water in front of him, the fish, like a new star that Mataichi had spotted, puffed out its chest with perfect composure and led a crowd of left-over goldfish in a glittering procession as the sun glinted gorgeous off its fins.

The Food Demon

They are called *kikujisa* in Japanese, but people who know food prefer to call them by their French name: endives. Ochiyo, the elder of the two sisters, had just rinsed and dried several of them, and they sat waiting on the chopping block in the middle of the room.

For an amateur's kitchen the room was equipped with an impressive array of cooking implements. It did, however, seem a little cramped.

The young cooking instructor, Besshirō, was leaning back in his chair with his cigarette hand frozen in mid-air, listening intently to the sounds coming in from outside. The early winter wind was starting to drown out the sounds of the city with its own sad racket, like an urban version of those tree-withering gales one reads about in classical poetry.

The younger sister, Okinu, had followed the older one around like a child and watched everything she did. But now she stood next to the chopping block, transfixed by the endives in the bamboo strainer. They were small, like bak choi shrunk to a size a little larger than a person's middle finger. They bulged charmingly in the middle and there was something precious about them that reminded one of the edible leaves of the butterbur plant.

The shape of a map that had spread into view as the water dripped from the strainer onto the wet wood surface of the still new chopping block was beginning to blur. Ochiyo had retrieved from rack, cupboard, and drawer every conceivable tool and spice container that might be called for and gingerly lined them up on the same surface, but she started to worry when the cooking teacher failed to move an inch even after she had finished. She stared meaningfully at her younger sister, who was better at communicating with him than she was, in the hope that she would send the signal that everything was ready. Okinu pretended not to notice.

The young cooking teacher threw his cigarette butt in the waste basket, stood up, and came over to the cutting board. He glanced at its surface and silently removed two or three unnecessary tools to the opposite side.

Then he transferred the endives from the strainer to a white porcelain bowl. There was an intentional swagger in his movements that made one think he was rough and careless. In his left hand he held a spoon above the bowl of endives. He added salt, pepper, and mustard. He added vinegar. When it came time to mix the vinegar in the spoon with a fork held in his right hand, he suddenly seemed charged with nervous energy. The prongs of the fork moved like the needle of a sewing machine in the narrow spoon. There was something mean-spirited about his dexterity that made people uneasy. Countless tiny wavelets covered the surface of the vinegar like a piece of crinkled silk crepe.

The younger sister Okinu cracked a smile at the contradiction he embodied. Besshirō kept his hands moving uninterrupted but glared at her out of the corner of his eye.

The older sister felt a chill go down her spine.

The vinegar in the spoon was scattered evenly over the endives.

The young cooking instructor held the spoon over the endives again and this time filled it with olive oil from the bottle.

'Three parts oil to one part vinegar.'

Pronouncing the proportions like a solemn proclamation, he sprinkled the three spoonfuls of olive oil over the endives and reverted to his arrogant, brusque and aloof manner. Dressing vegetables was a lot like applying make-up; you had to be careful not to ruin the freshness by slathering on too much. An over-dressed salad lacks refinement like a face smeared with too much foundation.

'The same goes for mixing batter.'

As if to prove his point, as Besshirō spoke he tossed the endives casually in the bowl. And yet his skill was apparent in the way they were dressed consistently from the bottom up. In the white porcelain bowl the lobes of the evenly oiled endives glinted sharply in the sunlight streaming through the windows.

The spiced vinegar had a powerful fragrance that seemed to intensify the visual effect of the pale yellow endives. It was bright and fresh like a spring day that has arrived while winter is still in full force.

Now Besshirō traded the spoon for a knife and quickly chopped the endives right in the bowl.

Identifying a nice piece he speared it with the fork and held it out to the older sister. 'Eat it,' he said, brandishing it more like a stage villain who has unsheathed his sword than someone offering a bite of food to taste.

Ochiyo drew back timidly and looked to her sister as if to ask her to take the lead.

'All right, you then.'

Besshirō held the fork out to the younger sister.

Okinu's throat twitched deep within her smooth neck. She looked at the fork from beneath her long eyelashes and once her pupils had focused on the morsel, she pinched it between her slightly rounded fingertips. The seed-shaped nostrils of her perky nose flared with hunger.

The piece of endive was chewed carefully in Okinu's mouth. Its fresh sourness melted as she swallowed and she felt her heart quicken with a deliciousness that left her mind blissfully vacant. A faint bitter taste lingered delightfully in the back of her mouth like the sliver of a new moon. This taste gently cleared away and made less odious the persistent memory of the meat she had eaten for lunch. The endive produced these effects even as it vanished easily in her mouth, imposing no burden of its own and leaving no residue behind.

'I hate to admit it, but it's delicious.'

Okinu spoke as she brought the back of her hand to the corner of her mouth, where a drop of saliva was beginning to form.

'Of course it's good. That's why I say hold the complaints until after you've had a taste!'

Besshirō's small eyes sparkled with pride.

'Even girls who normally have nothing good to say about people's cooking can't complain about mine. What do you think? Are you ready to admit defeat?'

Besshirō wouldn't let up.

Okinu gathered both of her sleeves up to her breast and, turning her back on the young cooking instructor, responded with a laugh in her voice, 'All right. Let's say you win.'

Seeing that the young cooking instructor and her sister, who normally had little to say to each other, had left off their argument lightheartedly and seemed inclined neither to continue their sparring nor to engage in a test of wills that might have deepened their connection to each other, Ochiyo breathed a bit easier. In her relief, she began to feel that she would like a taste as well.

'I suppose I might as well try a bite myself,' she said, as if she were talking about someone else. She extended the tips of her fingers to the bowl, plucked out a piece, and ate it.

'My word! That is delightful!'

Ochiyo emptied her expression and blushed slightly as she wiped her mouth with the edge of her apron. Okinu peered into the bowl of endives from over her sister's shoulder and said, 'Besshirō-san, put these away, would you? We'll have them for dinner.'

Besshirō, who was taking out a cigarette when he heard this, left it dangling from his mouth as he picked up the bowl, stuck out his elbows and emptied it into the garbage.

'Hey!'

'Food is like music. Do you really think it would stay this good until evening? It comes and it goes in a moment. That's what makes cooking the greatest of all the arts.'

Okinu gazed at the early spring colour of the endives still peeking out from the rubbish basket.

'You're so mean,' she said bitterly.

Glaring at the young cooking instructor she said, 'I'm going to tell Father.' Ochiyo too felt she could not remain silent and joined in the glare, placing a hand on her sister's shoulder.

The combined stare of all four of the young ladies' eyes proved too much for Besshirō and his own small ones blinked as he lowered his gaze. But his arrogance only worsened as he lit his cigarette with a swagger.

'If you really want to eat it, make it for yourselves tonight. But don't just copy what I did. Add something of your own. Even cooking requires originality.'

He threw the paper bag still containing endives on the cutting board in front of Okinu.

It was painful to watch this self-taught cooking instructor without a decent education try to pass himself off as an artist and go around expostulating his theories like this at the least provocation. But then again, one had to admit that he had certainly devoted himself body and soul to food. It was quite something to see him, so young, wearing a woman's apron and inspecting the pickle basins. Was he simply born with an extraordinary appetite for food? Or did he have some reason to think his survival depended on clinging to this instinct?

Bits and pieces of what Besshirō had said to her in the past came back to life in Okinu's mind.

'The world moves on and people change, but people's desire for food never changes.' 'There is nothing so honest as food. It lets you know if it's good or bad with a single bite.' 'Taste is a mystery.' One could say these things about the charms that bound any of the other human instincts to their objects, but when Besshirō said them he made it seem that they applied exclusively to the appetite and taste. The young man seemed crippled by his passion: all other instincts, sensibilities, and talents had been nipped in the bud so he could devote himself heart and soul to the taste of food. He never tasted anything while he cooked. His entire body served as the representative of his tongue and he seemed able to tell if the taste of what he was making was right simply by intuiting from the sequence and rhythm of its preparation. He was a freakish genius fated to make his contribution to human culture through the appetite alone. They say most geniuses are cripples. There was in fact something imbecilic about the beauty of this handsome young devotee of food, which reminded one equally of an unglazed vase and an artificial flower. It was as if his libido were so focused on eating that he was prevented from experiencing normal human emotions.

Once the talkative sister Okinu gave herself up to these thoughts, the connection between the three of them evaporated. Besshirō smoked furiously while slumping back in his chair and the elder sister Ochiyo, unable to bear the look on his face, busied herself timidly with putting away the cooking implements. For some moments one heard the striking sound of sand being blown onto the window glass.

'Some genius!' Okinu said, as if to herself. Then she looked him in the face. 'Imagine that. A man who's good at cooking!? What a vulgar kind of genius that is!' This was followed by an explosive peal of laughter, as if something pent up had been released.

Besshirō gave Okinu a sullen look, but managed to suppress the feelings that came surging up inside him.

'Well then! I guess I'll be going,' he said, getting up glumly as he took his hat from the corner of the stove where he had placed it and turned to the sisters, who had risen to see him off.

'I won't be seeing your father today. Please give him my best,' he said, and left through the service entrance.

Besshirō headed home through the early winter city, feeling the sand crunch between the soles of his shoes and the hard ground. There was quite a distance between the Keisetsu Villa, as the Araki family residence where he went to teach the sisters in Shiba no Adako was called, and his home in Nakabashi Hirokōji in Kyōbashi-ku. But he did not board the nearest train line, choosing to walk it slowly instead.

He did this partly because his finances were such that he needed to save even train fares, but also because he was free enough not to have to hurry. Besides that, he wanted to walk through the quirky area called Tunnel Lane.

It must have been left over from the rush to import Western things in the early Meiji period. A wide brick tunnel ran atop a small street, and people seemed to live on top of it like in a two-storey house. One could sometimes see children's clothing hanging out to dry on bamboo rods in the horizontal windows cut out of the walls beneath the tiled roofs.

The grey roof-tiles, the ochre walls, and the red bricks, all grimy with soot and exposure to the elements, had lost their original colours and always made Besshirō think that if they were flavours they would taste like black bread made with naked barley. The small, two-storey long houses built on both sides of this lifeless but gorgeous ruin had a darkish sliminess about them that reminded him of thrush innards pickled in salt. Besshirō was not making a special effort to translate the atmosphere of the area into the flavours of food, but whenever he came here he smelled naked barley and thrush innards still redolent of the nuts they had eaten. The great gingko trees of Sakuma-chō looked like brooms as they brushed the tops of the long houses.

During the short interval from the time he entered the lane and passed through the tunnel until it ended, and turned back onto the slightly wider avenue, he was able to forget his strange upbringing, his fiercely burning ambition, the frustrating world and his vexing current situation. It was a brief moment of detachment that came from a combination of the relief he felt from having finally sunk as far as possible in the world and a soul buoyed by an unrealistic sense of its own nobility. Was this what people called 'wabi'? As he passed through this neighbourhood he felt like a gentle and sincere person, so much so that he thought it must be manifest in his appearance. It would have been nice if he could have recaptured that sense of detachment simply by turning around and passing through the tunnel again, but this was not the case. The feeling came only once. If he turned back and strolled around the area again it seemed like nothing but a dirty mixture of Japanese and Western styles, a counterfeit town. For this reason he passed through it only once on his way to and from the Keisetsu Villa where he taught.

Crossing over the earthen bridge, he reached Nishi Nakadōri just as the town was beginning to light up for the night. Besshirō walked the remaining distance to his home in Nakabashi Hirokōji Dōri in a series of unnatural twists and turns. He would go out onto the main street only to turn back in to a side street and then cut in to an alley. Everywhere he looked there were food shops large and small. As he passed by their storefronts he would carefully scrutinise what special items they had put out to attract customers tonight.

One shop had red crabs and jumbo clams on display in the shadow of a *shōji* door bearing a crest. Another had a window filled with skewers of snipe, red beets, and parsley arranged on a plate.

'Everywhere you look it's the same old stuff. They're all idiots.'

As Besshirō mumbled this he felt both irritated and superior. If it were him… he thought, he would hunt down just the right items, things you wouldn't expect given the season.

The shopkeepers called out to him when he came into view, 'Sir! Come on in!'

But the greetings were superficial and made out of obligation; the shopkeepers had all been defeated by his biting lectures before.

'"Come in"? What the hell for? I wouldn't touch anything you're selling.'

'We are indeed a very *humble* establishment, Sir.'

He passed by many stores with this sort of exchange. It had become a habit for him to treat people haughtily to hide his lack of education. He knew that this repelled them eventually, but there was nothing he could do about it. He arrived home feeling a little lonely.

As he entered the alleyway between the clothing store and the *tatami* dealer he thought he heard the faint sound of small objects bouncing off the mud boards. Looking up into the darkened sky he felt something else small and cold brush his face past the bill of his old hat. 'Hail already?' he thought, and in an instant he saw his life of poverty, saddled with a child and an ordinary wife his aunt had forced upon him. The thought that he would have to face them after a few more steps filled him with more anger than annoyance. Suddenly he thought of the younger sister Okinu at the Keisetsu Villa. She was always making disparaging remarks with a look of contempt on her face, but she was also a mysterious creature who made a person dream of youthful poetry that was fine-grained and sad, supple and not to be written in words.

'Why can't I just be with her in a big mansion where we can live the way we want to? Who is it that gave people so many desires and then straight away refused to grant any of them? I don't know who it was that made this world, but I know I hate him.'

These angry thoughts came to him just as he crossed the threshold of his house, and they gave his voice a sharp edge of meanness when he spoke.

'Hey! Did you get the beer? You'd better not have forgotten it!'

His wife Itsuko, who sat facing her son under a five-candle-power bulb, feeding him one bite for every two she gave herself, hurriedly swallowed what she had been eating as if to keep him from seeing what was in her mouth. She wiped her mouth with her sleeve and came running over to him.

'Welcome home. Atsushi was hungry and kept crying so I went ahead and started eating and then I guess I lost track of the time. I'm sorry!'

As she said this she dispatched one last bit of food that had got caught between her rear molar and her cheek.

'I asked if you'd got the beer.'

'Yes, yes.'

Itsuko slung Atsushi, chopsticks in hand, onto her back and clattered off over the mud boards on Higashi Nakadōri to buy beer.

His face frozen into an expression on the verge either of exploding with anger or bursting into tears, Besshirō sat down cross-legged in front of the low table. It was scattered with a few plates and small bowls, and Itsuko's hastily abandoned rice bowl had spilled over on its side. The pitiful and disorderly scene, illuminated by the dim light of the lamp, looked as if some animal had been interrupted by an intruder just as it was devouring the scraps of food it had managed to scrape together.

'Good lord.'

Besshirō spat out the words and crossed his arms.

The Shi'insō house had been purchased by Okinu and Ochiyo's father Araki Keisetsu, a scholar of Chinese studies, when he was running the original Keisetsu-kan, a store selling sketchbooks and rubbings on Omote-dōri, just catty-corner to the house. He needed a place to stay over from time to time

66

since the living quarters of the store were quite small, so he had snapped it up as soon as it came on the market. It was simple and stylish, with a modest garden, and the twelve-mat main room had a *tokonoma* constructed of imported Chinese wood. After he bought the house Keisetsu's books, including a Chinese-Japanese dictionary, had sold very well, and being a good investor he was soon quite wealthy. So he sold the shop on Omote-dōri and had a mansion built with a view of Atago-yama to which he transferred the name 'Keisetsu Villa'. The Shi'insō house in the alley stood empty for a while, but when Besshirō insinuated himself into Keisetsu's household and became something like an employee of the Araki family, Keisetsu let him live there for free and paid him a nominal monthly allowance. There were, however, a few conditions. The house was to be kept clean. And the main room was to be used only sparingly. For this reason Besshirō and his wife confined themselves to the neighbouring six-mat room. When their son had been born in the autumn two years earlier, Keisetsu made a face at the thought that his house would be dirtied.

'He thinks he has the right to walk all over me just because of that paltry salary he pays me. I'll show him one of these days.'

But he had no idea how he would do this. And the more he thought about it the more miserable his situation seemed.

He clucked his tongue and looked back down at the table. He kept his hands tucked inside his sleeves and his palms pressed against his bloated belly while a grumbling sound escaped from the pit of his stomach.

'Let's see what those two were eating.'

A boiled sweet potato stuck with a few grains of rice teetered on the edge of a shallow dish.

'What's this? They're eating potatoes. The poor wretches.'

Besshirō had a look of utter contempt on his face, but he was made to feel a little better by the thought that his wife was obeying his commandment that they eat only inexpensive food.

'Well, well, well. Let's see how she prepared it.'

He brushed the rice off the potato and popped it into his wide-open mouth. It was surprisingly well cooked.

'Not bad. Nothing to sneeze at.'

Besshirō made an uncomfortable face.

Itsuko came back with hail sticking to her bangs. Her son in one hand, she held out two bottles of beer with the other.

'Here's two for now. They said they'd send the boy over later with the rest.'

Besshirō had always told his wife if he was drinking one beer she should have three others ready at hand. This was the only way for him to enjoy the first one with gusto and without restraint. If he was drinking the only beer in the house this fact would gnaw at him and keep him from being able to relax and get his money's worth of pleasure out of it. It was a waste to drink it that way. And bottled beer didn't go bad, so you might as well have some extras around. Itsuko's beer order at the shop was in accord with Besshirō's instructions.

'That'll do fine,' he said.

He ordered her to serve his dinner in the main room. This was a rarity.

'But what if we accidentally spill something?' she said, making a show of concern. But her husband just raised his eyebrows and said nothing in reply. Thinking she had best not spoil his good mood, Itsuko strapped her son to her back and started to prepare the main room.

The *tatami* were entirely covered with protective paper treated with persimmon, and the ornamental screens, the scrolls hanging from the rafters, and even the objects in the *tokonoma* were cloaked in dust covers. It was as if the objects in the room

68

considered the family to be of an alien race and, believing that even to be seen or touched by them was a desecration, had agreed to protect themselves at all costs. Itsuko found it hateful, an all-too-brazen reminder of the inhumanity of their owner Keisetsu.

With a slight thrill of revenge she tore off every one of the coverings. She put a handkerchief over her son's face to protect his nose and eyes and gave the room a good dusting. Sensing her husband's mood, she even switched out the bulb for a fifty-candlepower one. As she stood in the now brilliantly illuminated room, Itsuko looked around herself and felt her spirits rise for the first time in ages. But she was a timid woman, and soon the thought that they were doing something wrong behind the landlord's back made her unable to enjoy the view. She put out the cushions and the beer and then returned to her interrupted meal with her son in the smaller room.

Besshirō, who had been making a racket in the kitchen while all of this was going on, opened the sliding screen and brought out a portable stove and a ceramic hotpot. Then came a nicely arranged lacquer tray holding a bowl heaped with something white, a dish containing brown lumps of something else, a plate with another white object, and some pickles. He brought out a tray with a soy sauce container, a dish of salt, and a chinaware spoon. Lastly he grabbed a bottle opener and a glass with one hand, stuck his elbows out in a stiff pose like a samurai entering a room, and tore off the queer apron from around his waist and hurled it back into the kitchen. He closed the sliding screen and walked around the room to the porch, where he threw open the glass doors. The dark garden was lit up by the light bulb, making the little artificial mountain and pond stand out in relief, as a small flurry of hail brushed past on the way down. Luckily there was no wind so although it was cold the flame of the stove and the brazier stayed steady.

As he sat cross-legged on the cushion and took the beer in his hand, he smiled and called out through the wall.

'Hey! Would you do me a favour and keep that kid from crying tonight?'

He brought his lips to his first cup of beer and drank it down, belching loudly with pleasure as he wiped the foam from his lips with his palm. On the other side of the wall his wife Itsuko imagined him playing around like a *rakugo* storyteller as he drank his beer with exaggerated gusto.

He reached out for the lid of the ceramic hotpot and let out a whooping yell as he held it high in the air. The smell of boiled daikon came steaming out mixed with the fragrance of the broth.

'Preparations are complete! Now behold the results!' he intoned, but the lid was too hot and Itsuko could picture him hopping around as he quickly dropped it on the floor.

'Ah! Tatatatatatata!'

He seemed to have put the lid down right on the *tatami*. Would it be damaged by the moisture? Itsuko put the thought out of her mind and found herself amused instead. She tittered quietly. Her husband was always arrogant to others and tyrannical towards his own family. But when he was working with food he was innocent and childlike. She was touched, but she transferred that feeling to her child, whom she had let sleep next to her to keep him from crying. She put a hand between his kimono and his cotton-stuffed jacket and pulled him towards her. He had just fallen asleep and his little body was warm and more flexible than usual.

In the main room Besshirō was drinking his beer accompanied by an array of dishes made with daikon. All he had in the kitchen was a single ordinary Nerima daikon, but he had prepared a whole menu from it in the *ichiju-sansai*, or 'one soup and three sides', format. For the raw component he grated the daikon. For the simmered dish he cut the daikon into round slices and boiled them with bonito flakes. The grilled plate he did with daikon carved into small fish shapes and the hotpot counted for the soup.

For him it was a perfect rendition of an *ichiju-sansai* menu.

There were some things he was quite particular about. If the food was fancy he would be satisfied with just one dish, but when it came to more humble items he required formal beauty. He had always admired what he had heard about the lifestyle of Fukuchi Gen'ichirō, the Meiji-era advocate of 'civilisation and enlightenment' who later in life wrote plays for the great kabuki actor Danjurō IX. Fukuchi was a former retainer of the Shōgun and a true Tokyoite who even in the most dire poverty would serve the simple ingredients he had available as a full *ichiju-sansai* menu. For the grilled item he often used cheap items such as slices of salted salmon.

Besshirō had collected a number of true stories and anecdotes involving food from various cooks while preaching to them in his arrogant way. Having more memory than he had originality, he would often draw on this knowledge to spin stories of his own.

He surveyed his perfectly arranged tray as he alternated sips of beer with bits of boiled daikon dipped in a mixture of soy sauce and *ponzu*. He knew the stories surrounding this dish as well. It was the favourite of Prince Saionji Kinmochi. When he had first heard this, he was surprised that the Prince, who was a man of taste as well as a politician, would have arrived finally at such a simple flavour. It was unexpected, but it somehow made sense as well. He always tried to sample the foods that important people ate. This was partly the result of his hero worship and partly his way of sussing out important people. He felt that the most straightforward and simple way of judging character was to try a person's favourite foods and work backwards from there.

The broth for the hotpot was seasoned with his own original vegetable extract prepared in advance. It was early winter so the daikon was just starting to fatten up. With his chopsticks he chose one particularly nice piece from among the eight or nine gingko-shaped pieces that had floated to the surface on the foam. He dipped a corner of it in a small dish of thick *tamari* soy sauce, blew on it to cool it off, and ate it. Each soft and delicate bite melted in his mouth with the unassuming taste of natural ingredients picked fresh and in season. It had the rough fragrance typical of root vegetables. But it was surprisingly sweet.

'Extraordinary!' he marvelled aloud to himself.

Now he began eating in earnest, taking each morsel as it floated to the surface, cooling it down, and popping it into his mouth. It was more like sucking than eating. He looked like a ravenous mole.

From time to time his chopsticks ventured into the bowl with the grated daikon, but he never made it to the plate of boiled daikon.

He finished eating with a look of total satisfaction on his face and looked out at the hail as he shut off the stove.

Besshirō felt the effects of alcohol quite easily and now he propped his left arm on his knee as he sat cross-legged to try to stabilise his wobbly torso. Earlier he had belched loudly to express his satisfaction, but now it was the real thing as the food he had eaten began to stimulate the slack walls of his distended stomach. Now and then he felt bitter globs of food being coughed up into his mouth, including unchewed bits of daikon. It was his habit to belch like this after a meal and then to further ruminate whatever came out, even with other people present. 'It's started again,' thought Itsuko, mortified that there would

72

be nothing she could do to stop Atsushi from imitating his father once he got used to seeing him do this at family meals.

The belching was unpleasant, but when he drank beer and smoked cigarettes to make it less so, he felt an unreal and beautiful anxiety in his body. He often said to Itsuko, 'Right now I feel like a normal person who loves his wife and child.' And Itsuko would think doubtfully, as she tucked her son into bed, 'So at other times he feels like the snapping turtle that Keisetsu nicknamed him for!'

Besshirō felt normal as he smoked and enjoyed the sight of the hail falling in the garden. It was late and the darkness was deepening. The board fence around the garden was not visible so the darkness seemed to extend forever into the horizon. Illuminated by the light of the bulb, the miniature mountain and the lush trees, the pond and the garden grasses looked like nothing more than a little stage-set of thin metal plates and outlines traced in wire. It was a darkness that could only swallow and never spit things up. What would happen to a person who got caught in this horrifically dark, dull and boundless digestive force? You could cry and scream but never outrun it. And gradually your body would dissolve like an insect caught in a sundew plant. Knowing that you would be consumed you could do nothing about it except squeal as you were taken. Forever – Besshirō did sometimes try to imagine what death would be like. He was born with the burden of something inside him that he could not handle and he had thrust it on the world in the hope that at least someone would understand. But they had no time for him and threw it right back at him. He sprang into action like a samurai. People thought he was insane and ducked out of his way. He tried every move he knew. And when he was utterly worn out from being rejected by the world, bitter and heavy in body and soul with only an itchy twinge of pain remaining, he thought of death. It would settle everything. When he braced himself for death and looked back on his life he would think, 'That's all there was to it,' and give up easily. A wry smile of resignation came to his lips. No one as intense as he was could possibly have managed to survive until almost thirty without thinking about death from time to time.

The death that he imagined when he had looked back on his life and given it up, saying, 'That's all there was to it,' made life seem like a flimsy thing. If that's all there was to life then there wasn't much to death either. Besshirō liked to say pedantic things even though he was supposed to lack the education and brainpower necessary for deep thinking.

This way of thinking about life and death was the result of experiences that had been forced upon him, and there was no changing it now. As a young man he had learned how to make copy-books for calligraphy practice. They included phrases like 'LIFE AND DEATH ARE ONE' or 'LIFE IS BUT FOAM AND FROTH,' which he had understood in this sense. In the end he had simply decided, 'I may as well have something good to eat.' What was the point in putting on a show to impress people?

But the oozing darkness tonight was suffused with a mysterious power that made it different from the easily accepted death he had imagined. It was inexorable and insatiable like the emptiness of despair combined with cruel love; it would take whatever it grabbed hold of and lick it until it dissolved, only to give birth to it again in its original form and repeat the process over and over without ever being satisfied. Could such a force really exist in the world? Besshirō had devoured many foods in his life, and he felt that each one of them had its own volition and strength which made it what it was. This was true even of things other than food, as long as they had taste of some sort. So what about the taste of this darkness? Nothing could have been a better symbol of eternity and repetition. Human beings never tire of the foods they like, no matter how much of them they eat. Maybe the hunger of the darkness was like that.

It was like the appetite of the universe. Next to it the human appetite seemed like nothing.

'Damn,' he mumbled.

For the first time in quite a while he recalled his awful past.

He was born as the only son of the head priest of a prominent temple in Kyoto, but he lost his father when he was still quite young. His mother was his father's second wife, but they had never officially married, and the temple had its own squabbles, the result of which was that a stranger was brought in as his father's successor. The mother and child were thrown out unceremoniously with nothing but the clothes on their backs. His father had a reputation as a great priest who had transcended worldly desires, and all of this was the result of his distaste for practical matters, but for some reason Besshirō's mother did not resent him for it.

'The man was like a child. How could anyone blame him?' she said. And then she told him what his father had said when Besshirō was born. 'I'm old and I might not be there when this kid starts to be conscious of the world. He might suffer without me and hate me for bringing him into this accursed world when he never asked for it. But you tell him it was the same with me. I didn't ask to be born into this world of suffering and be a burden to my parents. So we're even.' These words seemed cold, but they also left a strange echo in Besshirō's heart that coldness alone could not explain.

In the beginning they had moved from one temple to another, staying with his father's former disciples who now had their own temples and wanted to do something for them out of loyalty to their late mentor. But that did not last long. In each temple there were always family members who made them feel

75

uncomfortable. The last place they stayed was the home of an old man who made rubbings for a living and had been his father's partner at *go*. He was poor, but he was a widower, which made things easier. His mother took care of the old man's cooking and laundry and, since Besshirō had just graduated from junior high school, it was decided that he would be apprenticed to the old man, making copy-books for calligraphy practice. The man was a strange old bird. He would spend several nights out when he played *go*, and when the elementary school athletic meets started in the spring and fall he was almost never home. He would seek them out all over Kyoto, and in the suburbs as well, and come home talking excitedly about the perfectly synchronised exercises at this school or the runner at that one who was faster than any he had seen before.

During these absences Besshirō would make albums in the workshop that smelled of glue. There were, of course, variations in the colour of the ink, but whether you called it a 'cicada wing' or a 'golden crow' it was really just black: a melancholy black, like the past visualised, which was never going to colour a living thing again. The characters that emerged written in this black from out of the cold white expanse of the paper were too bleak for the young Besshirō to take. 'Now that the rain's let up why don't you head down to the river and catch us some small-fry and we can make ourselves a nice dinner,' said his mother as she repaired some item of clothing. Besshirō took a bamboo colander and headed over the embankment and down to the river.

At that time there were still small fish in the Kamo river. Depending on the season you could find *gori*, *kawahaze*, and *hae* fish. And just after it rained the carp and the eel came to the surface so you could reap quite a bounty. A group from the neighbourhood had already arrived and were making a ruckus as they splashed around after the fish. On the opposite bank a family out picking grasses had come all the way down to the water's edge. And people sporting parasols were also gathering around where the embankment splits off and heads to Kurama. Besshirō's hard life had made him shy, so he avoided the crowds and found a spot to fish in a small branch of the river, where he was shielded by the embankment and the profusion of budding willows. The wild violets smelled sweet and the Tadasu Forest was blanketed in mist. When he realised he was crying and shut his eyes, the tears fell with a pling as if onto a scrap of tin. But he was good with his hands and managed despite the tears to catch a handful of fish in no time. He brought them back, his mother prepared them skilfully, and mother and son shared the meal in the thin light of the early spring evening in someone else's house.

His mother did not like speaking about her background with her son. But he knew that she was picky about food and had to have something fishy, even in the mornings, before she would touch her rice. As if to excuse herself for this behaviour she would say, 'What do you expect? I was brought up spoiled rotten in a city of gourmands!'

Besshirō was able to gather a few things about his mother's past by asking other people. In the heart of Osaka's prestigious Senba district there lived the owner of an old establishment who was a devout follower of Besshirō's father. As a result of a bizarre series of unfortunate events, the shop went bank-rupt and its owner got sick and died, leaving behind his only daughter. Besshirō's father had looked after the man right up to the end, and even helped out with money in a clumsy way, but to no avail. The shop owner, for his part, had resigned himself to his fate as the result of bad karma. But in order to expiate his sins and to repay Besshirō's father, who had recently lost his wife and become a widower, he sent his daughter up to the temple, whereupon he expired. Besshirō's mother, who said so little about other things, would sometimes let slip this reflection: 'Here I am, a person who was sent to the temple for the purpose of expiating somebody's sins, and I can't free myself from the desire for food. I feel terrible about it, but maybe there was just too much bad karma. And now it can't be helped.' She never gave up her hunt for food, although in her mind she kept it to a minimum.

When Besshirō was a teenager people started asking him to help out at elegant gatherings. In this old capital where every inhabitant considered himself a person of taste, people were always gathering to practise the so-called 'four arts' of *koto*, *go*, painting and calligraphy. It started with him going to help out at showings by antique dealers who were the old man's clients, but before long he was quite in demand. There was something about this young man, whose cleverness was tempered by shyness, that caught people's attention. The white skin visible from his full-cheeked face to his chest was the colour of cherry blossoms and had the smell and texture of young leaves. The cultured crowd enjoyed the sight of him officiating at one of their gatherings, decked out in clothes made from the old man's old-fashioned kimono and *hakama*. They jokingly christened him 'Sen no Yoshirō' after the childhood name of Sen no Rikyū, the founder of the tea ceremony. No one knows whether the young Rikyū was as attractive as Besshirō, but the famous story of how he swept a garden clean only to scatter it again with autumn leaves certainly makes one think that this prodigy of taste must have been a beauty as well. Besshirō was quite pleased with the nickname, and even started to use it himself, with no little pride.

He liked this helper's job in which he got to eat elegant bento boxes and even earn a little money here and there. After consuming two such bentos and being invited for a cup of *matcha* tea, he slipped through to the other side of the red-and-white-striped curtain that had been put up in the hall, and sat down for a rest on a veranda overlooking a garden. The sun shone so brilliantly that it seemed to drip from every young leaf in the garden. And the surface of the veranda too was thoroughly bright and warm. He lay down on his back, stretched out his arms and legs and dozed off as he rubbed his full stomach. The noon bells of the Chion-in and Shōgo-in Temples were still ringing. The thirty-six peaks of Higashiyama stood out softly on the horizon, frowning slightly as a summer mist drew over them. There was no one else on the veranda with him. But there was a constant rumble of people passing through the central corridor leading from a waiting room in a separate complex to the stage, as if a wheeled shrine were being trundled back and forth. In the waiting room they seemed to have started preparing for the afternoon performance and the sounds came spilling out of a *koto* and a *kokyū* being tuned with a *shakuhachi*. Also in the mix was the nasal voice of a blind man and the youthful laughter of girls.

The young Besshirō found pleasure in this brief interval in which he was peripherally aware of all of these sights and sounds even as he continued to doze off, unbothered by it all. As he lay with the sun on his belly, he felt the richness of the food he had eaten as it was absorbed into his body and seemed to exude from his every pore. He felt extravagant, as if his body itself were a costly commodity. Trapped in this luxurious flesh, the awful thoughts that were always with him were transformed into nothing more than an internal spice. There was a pleasant sweet smell that made him think there must be a plot of peonies in the garden somewhere.

The sky over the old capital was a cloudless pale blue. A single cloud passed gently by towards friendly eyelashes and full breasts. It floated right into his dream as he napped and became a bird that flew off on glossy white wings. Oh! the sorrow of early summer! 'Yoshirō-san! What are you doing sleeping in a place like this? There's work to be done you know. Wake up, sleepyhead.' Someone pinched his nose. They were the soft supple fingers of a woman in her prime.

Gradually Besshirō stopped coming home. He much preferred distracting himself by going from party to party full of young girls and lively fun to staying in the old man's miserable hovel with only his mother for company, who had become like the hungry ghost of a court lady. One thought had firmly implanted itself in his heart. He knew that his livelihood was endangered without some kind of skill, some calling that would make him superior to others. The anxiety this caused him was like a searing flame that made him unable to sit or stand for worry, and was only made worse by that awful irritation that he had bottled up inside him. The more he felt its scorching heat the more he thrust himself into the motley and changing world in the hope that he could scratch it off on his surroundings. During this period his natural talents allowed him to acquire more than an amateur's competence in most of the arts of the cultured world. Before long he was 'that handy Yoshirō', welcomed at the home of every master. At the school for *go* he partnered with beginners and at the *koto* master's house they never had to pay to have the *koto* tuned. He got the flowers ready for the young misses at the school for flower arranging and he gave good advice on how to make tea and handle the dishes to the girls and the married ladies studying the tea ceremony. Having learned the techniques of mounting and printing in his training with the old man, he would mount scrolls and carve wooden seals for anyone who asked. For the characters he copied Song Dynasty calligraphy. Painting was his strongest suit and sometimes he even thought he might make a career of it.

He could do anything people asked of him. Who wouldn't welcome such a handy helper?

And so he went from place to place without ever getting too involved, fending off the gloom of each day. His mother had left him alone on the assumption that he was out in the world to study and that success would come any day now, and while the old man grumbled about having lost his helper, he never brought it to the level of a scolding.

The masters of the various arts and their senior disciples made him part of their entourage and brought him along to eat at the Tawara-ya, the Hisago-tei, and all the other top restaurants in Kyoto. He never lacked for the best cuisine and he had a preternatural gift for intuiting its most profound secrets.

At some point during all of this Besshirō suddenly noticed something: he was welcome everywhere but never once had he felt respected. He thought quite highly of himself in private. He had been the scion of a great temple, when he was young at least, and his mother had passed on to him her poise and refinement as the daughter of an old merchant family. There was something mortifying about being treated as 'that handy Yoshiro'. He began to feel that this must be the source of a good part of those scorching fires that burned within him. Somehow he had to find a way to get people to call him 'Sensei'.

Mixing in the world had rid him of almost all of his shyness and this new desire that now reared its head within him spurred him on even more. He learned how to manipulate people with a haughty attitude, to disdain and look down his nose at them. He learned how to be critical of everything and promote himself above all else. And he became vain about his looks. He took out a hand-held mirror, studied his appearance, and despaired. The young man reflected there was far too young and beautiful. He lacked the gravitas to be called 'Sensei'. He made an effort to be stern and grown-up sounding when he spoke. The weaker of his associates were taken aback by this sudden transformation and shied away from him. The stronger ones were offended and cursed him for it. 'Our handy helper seems to be forgetting his place!' And the only people who called him Sensei were the chefs.

'Yoshirō has changed.' 'He's gone crackers on us.' Such was the consensus in the world of sophisticates. He did have a sweet girlfriend who had lodged in his heart like a dayflower, but she wilted under these rumours and it was not to be.

Once a young man has let himself indulge in this sort of exaggerated high and mighty behaviour it is not an easy thing to step back and contemplate a more subtle approach. The reputation he had gained was not what he had intended, but he knew where it came from. It was because he lacked a proper education, however painful and galling it was to admit. He felt a wave of self-pity come over him as he thought of how his circumstances had kept him from continuing his education. It made him bitter. But identifying the source of that bitterness in order somehow to overcome it was much too complex a problem for him to manage at that age. There was no point in lamenting it. He might be behind but the only choice was to study in secret and catch up. He tried hard to read books. But for someone who had already drawn his conclusions about the world through smarts, instincts, and hard knocks, their tedious argumentation seemed circuitous and condescending. He felt sleepy as soon as he opened one. When he made an effort to read on, his head ached with the dreariness of it and he was constantly distracted by thoughts of food. He got up and went out to look for something good to eat.

In the end his only choice was to build on what he could learn by watching and listening. But this time he modified his method. Instead of listening humbly and gleaning what he could, now he would go in swinging and take it. Did he want respect that badly? Absolutely. Before he began consciously to find relief in food, the possibility of being called 'Sensei' had meant more to him than having a girlfriend. He lost many friends thanks to this new method. But he was also taken under the wings of a few eccentrics. There is, after all, a kind of friendship that actually improves, like Chinese music, with the addition of clanging gongs and crashing cymbals. He fell in with an older crowd of men whose hard lives had sheathed their hearts in callouses.

One of these men was the owner of a modern European-style restaurant in Kyōgoku called 'Maison Higaki'. Having lived in the United States, he had an obsession with art and the lives of artists and painted in oils when he was not managing his restaurant. The room where he slept over in the restaurant was like a painter's atelier. He loved to buttonhole his customers and tell them about the culture of Greenwich Village in New York. It was a neighbourhood that tried to mimic the art districts of Paris, and its peculiar charm came from a combination of the American mentality of its inhabitants and the exaggeration that comes from admiration. He spoke with the passion of an apostle, and he designed his restaurant to approximate his ideal. There were evenings of bacchanalia and rooms with blue candles. It was an obvious gathering place for artists and young men with modern tastes. The young people found the old capital oppressive and took extreme measures to liberate themselves from it. This was the reason people gave that the modernism of Kyoto was so much more jarring and intoxicating than its Tokyo counterpart .

Besshirō became a regular. Both he and the owner had seen through the other's weakness in terms of basic knowledge, so they were able to engage in high-spirited discussions without worry. Once they started talking there was no stopping them. When one of them defeated the other in an argument he would bare his teeth in derision. But each was thrilled to have found an opponent with whom he could butt heads freely and let loose with all the strength he had. They also enjoyed finding cunning ways to steal the other's knowledge and wrest away his advantages. While Besshirō extolled the austere refinement of the Orient, the owner of the Maison Higaki took pride in the bold appeal of Western tastes. Thus they traded knowledge and each tucked what he learned away in his bag of tricks.

One thing they always agreed on was the supremacy of art. Having been brought up among the lower classes by mistake, they clung to art as the only means by which they could use their instincts to elevate themselves to their rightful place. They were immensely proud of the depth and breadth of their discernment. And in this regard they trusted each other. They were unstinting in their praise of each other's ability to appreciate and critique everything from the 'four arts' of high society, to women, theatre, ceramics, food, and philosophy. 'We're a couple of geniuses!' 'Geniuses indeed!'

The owner of the Maison Higaki had a chronic chest ailment. For this reason he had never married, but one sensed that he had a very powerful libido from the whiff of the erotic in his oil paintings and in the bibelots he collected. His tall, gaunt body was covered in black and blue patches and was always gasping on the inside with the pain of unfulfilled desires. Compared to this, Besshirō was of average height, but otherwise had an extremely robust physique that could easily withstand the indulgence of all sorts of sensual desires. With the exception of one particular craving, he was able to satisfy his desires well enough to remain detached.

Higaki took Besshirō with him to enjoy pleasures both refined and risqué, from the terraces along the Kamogawa where people cool off in the evening to the dark-red shadows beneath the lanterns of the Miyagawa-chō geisha district. In the midst of these leisured pursuits the two of them presented an extraordinary contrast: one was gloomy with frustration over his inability to enjoy it all, and the other blissfully and brightly detached thanks to his ability to do so. In the owner's gloominess Besshirō sensed both the baseness and the depth of the older man's appetites, while the latter envied and marvelled at the strength of Besshirō's body. Each was secretly dazzled by the other.

While they had their ups and downs and did keep a few secrets, the two men respected each other, and the bond between them gradually strengthened like two ropes entwined together. Because of their origins as tradesmen they both felt intimidated by the intelligentsia, so the scowling youth and the man in his prime isolated themselves within their own class of two. They were ideal partners in the pleasure of heaping abuse on anyone who had the temerity to try to intimidate them. And before long they felt bereft if they did not see each other every day.

Besshirō was the precise opposite of Higaki in his stress on the profundity and nobility of Oriental art, but when the latter hit him back with a reproduction of one of his masterpieces of Western art, he took it in without hesitation. Most of what the older man had brought back from abroad were works of modern French masters whose permissiveness in terms of instinct, sensuality, enjoyment, and even physical lust were astonishing for someone who had only been allowed the slightest glimpses of such things through the constraints of Oriental discipline and morals. Besshirō was embarrassed by what struck him as their shameless openness. And while he made noises to Higaki about how amateurish they were, his sensuous side rejoiced at having found an outlet.

He enjoyed Western cuisine, and ate much more of it now at the restaurant. And he learned many useful and interesting things from its owner about Western culture and lifestyle.

Besshirō took the insights and knowledge that he had gained and returned to the trade in which he had been brought up. He preached *dessin* to the pack of calligraphers and ink painters and dropped the names of Van Gogh and Cezanne. He explained the 'tea party' and the virtues of the aperitif to the practitioners of tea and flower arrangement, peppering his speech with French words like '*composition*' and '*nuance*'.

Of course all of this existed in Oriental art as well, having emerged by necessity through practice. It was just the terms and traditions that were different. For that reason everything that Besshirō said made sense to his listeners, and while the more sensitive among them wondered if that was all there was to Western culture after all, the tendency in those days to look to the West for novelty and modernity meant that while they might criticise him behind his back for affecting Western manners, when they met him face to face they felt obliged to sound him out for new ideas. He regained his popularity. He suggested some fairly radical things, such as allowing for encores after a performance of Japanese music, or placing flower arrangements around nude statues, but he managed to gain enough influence to get people to do things that only a very few had tried before, such as conducting a tea ceremony with a table and chairs, or including a few Western dishes in a *kaiseki* menu. Here and there people started calling him 'Sensei'.

Fuelled by this momentum, Besshirō plunged into the society of young artists who gathered at the Maison Higaki. But his arrogance and rough manners did not go over well with the skittish young intellectuals. Just when he thought he had charmed and talked circles around them, he would sense the silent wall of their rejection. It was hard to put his finger on what it was, but it had the unnerving power to destroy effortlessly the courage he needed to enter into the society of modern young men. He had no choice but to rethink.

It was an evening in spring. A party was being held on the second floor of the Maison Higaki. A female *waka* poet and scholar of Buddhism had been invited to Kyoto to lecture at a girls' school run by a certain Buddhist sect, and the party was in her honour. Her painter husband was also in attendance. The formal speeches were over quickly and the atmosphere was relaxed and intimate. But Besshirō had read about this woman in magazines and there was something about her that he found irritating. She was preaching Buddhism to the artists, saying that people who make art are often inspired by religion. But her proselytising made him feel that she was taking the side of the temple that had made him so miserable when he was a child. Before long he had inserted himself into the conversation and started to criticise her in a voice laden with irony. The woman's appearance, like a girl who had grown into a woman without ageing or knowing any hardship, made him want to bully her all the more.

Her face registered a flash of annoyance at his rudeness, but she swallowed her anger and replied, 'Oh no! I would never want to force it on anyone who felt they didn't need it.' Besshirō responded to this in a rage while the woman declared repeatedly that she had no intention of answering anyone who spoke to her like that. To Besshirō she seemed like a naive little girl digging her heels in.

The party had ground to a halt for a moment, but the void was soon filled by the sounds of pleasant conversation, and people ceased to notice Besshirō, who sat there scowling with his arms crossed and looking aggrieved. His anger seemed to have filled every part of his body down to the tips of the long wavy hairs on his head. And to make matters worse, the others had asked her to sing 'The Four Seasons of the Capital' or some such song and she seemed to have obliged just to aggravate him. She kept her voice quiet but she was relaxed and clearly enjoying herself. Her husband was clapping time with the rest of the room.

Everything felt like a personal insult to Besshirō. He resolved to shut this woman down and restore his own dignity by any means possible. He made a point of speaking about the owner's collection of paintings, caught the woman and her husband as they were leaving and urged them to drop by the studio for a look. The room also contained a number of Besshirō's works.

Making a show of humility, he badgered the woman to critique his work. There were several framed specimens of ink paintings with calligraphy in seal-style characters. The woman seemed to like this sort of thing and began to examine them in earnest. But then she turned around to her husband and said, 'You know Papa, these are very prettily made. But don't you think they're more tasteful than anything else?'

The husband had a look of pity on his face and said, 'I'm afraid so. They don't go much beyond tasteful.' Besshirō guffawed and tried to look unconcerned, but inside he felt cut to the quick for the first time in his life. The husband proclaimed that the work was 'continental', whatever that meant, and then even his friend the owner of the Maison Higaki was displaying his dimples in agreement with the woman's assessment. 'I do believe it's true! Your art *is* tasteful.' How mortifying.

Besshirō was devastated but also perverse, and decided secretly to plan another attack on the woman. Since the couple were planning to look around Kyoto and enjoy the spring weather for another five or six days, Besshirō offered to make lunch for them. If this woman was going to reduce his art so cavalierly to the category of the 'tasteful', then he needed to know how much she understood about taste. And the best way to test her was with food. No doubt she had never eaten anything better than the sorts of things that ladies of leisure cook at home or standard restaurant fare. If he discovered that she had no taste he could dismiss her criticism of his art. On the other hand, if she did turn out to have taste, she couldn't fail to be impressed by his cooking. In this way he felt sure that he could defeat her and force her to recognise his talents.

Luckily, the couple accepted his invitation.

For the venue he borrowed a tea room on the Kamo River, attached to the home of an acquaintance who was a tea master. With the help of an apprentice chef and a couple of serving girls he began preparations for a feast for the couple.

He had taken careful note on the evening of the party of what the woman ordered and what she seemed to enjoy. From time to time he had even asked her directly. None of this was conscious or intentional on his part. It was simply the working of his bloodhound's nose and his instinctual interest in other people's appetites. He had not been able to establish whether the woman's taste was that of an amateur or a professional. But he did have a sense of the kinds of food she craved.

Ignoring traditional menu protocols and freely mixing Japanese, Chinese, and Western foods, Besshirō planned dishes that he felt would satisfy these cravings. As he worked he felt a rare flood of love and affection for other people. It was no longer about winning or losing. And his conqueror's lust had faded as well.

If he could just make that overgrown girl's eyes widen with pleasure as she took in with all five senses a satisfaction greater than any in the human world, what an achievement that would be for cooking itself! His own existence ceased to matter. It was with this feeling in his heart that he shelled crabs out-of-season because she had said she liked them and kneaded tiny portions of soba noodles in the Matsue style. Suddenly he remembered the feeling he had had when, as a sensitive child, he would wake up crying in the night asking for *hōraimame* candies, and his father the elderly priest would waddle into the dark town to buy them for him. Besshirō tilted his face away from the kneading board to keep the tears from hitting it. Wasn't cooking an act of love? And wasn't that love best spent on children and half-wits?

But Besshirō proceeded on the assumption that the woman was a connoisseur and busied himself ordering foods that could stand up to a connoisseur's scrutiny, like *moroko* fish straight from the Moroko River in Sakamoto, and pepper tree bark from Kurama.

The woman looked impressed and thanked him as she began to eat. 'This catfish roe is gorgeous!' 'And the stewed *ebi imo* potatoes are exquisite!' As her lips took on a coat of oil from the *kara-age*, she said simply 'Delicious!' 'Delicious!' and ate on single-mindedly. Besshirō had worked himself up into a frenzy and now that the dishes he had fretted over so much were being consumed one after another with such abandon, he felt a wave of exhaustion.

The woman had a voracious appetite, but her husband the painter was even more voracious. He ate every last bite and said, with a *sencha* tea-cup in hand, 'That was superb. I have to tell you that *this* is your true art.' Then he turned to his wife and smiled as if to solicit her agreement and say that he meant this positively and not ironically. The woman smiled as well, but when she spoke her voice was serious. 'I could not agree more. It is not a figure of speech when I say that this meal was a true work of art.'

Besshirō knew that he had hit the bull's-eye, but at the same time his heart sank. No matter how he might try to finesse it there was no denying the dreary common sense of the world that considered any one of the four elegant arts to be more prestigious than cooking, and held that their practitioners were most appropriately called 'Sensei'. On the day of the party, his attempt at the high had been merely 'tasteful', and today the low was praised as art. It made no difference whether it was about inborn talent or acquired cultivation. He couldn't win either way. What could he say?

The Kamo River was slightly swollen and its cloudy current spilled over its banks and split off into tiny rivulets. The flower petals and other plant matter that collected behind the gabions were the same as they had always been, but there were fewer fish than before and no children out trying to catch them. The mid-spring sky came in and out of view through the budding branches of the willows along the embankment.

For a time he listened intently in the silent room to the sound of the river's rushing water, and thought back to his childhood. The house he grew up in was concealed by a bamboo forest on the far side of the river, but he pictured his lonely mother in his mind. She continued to obsess over food, like a hungry ghost, as she waited for her son to come home having figured out some way, any way, of making a living. He had not been home for a while, but the old man would still be out looking for elementary school athletic meets, hoping that the sight of the children's artless games would help him forget the advance of old age.

Besshirō covered his emotions with laughter as he told the story of how he had come to the banks of this river as a child to catch small fish for dinner with his mother. 'I have eaten all sorts of delicious foods since then, but nothing has ever been as good as that fish dinner was.' And then, reflecting on what he had felt today as well, he said, 'I suppose the difference between taste and art has to do with the presence or absence of love.'

The woman did not respond to this immediately, but first told of their experience at a famous Parisian restaurant called Foyot during a trip abroad. The dining room of this restaurant was outfitted to be as quiet as possible: the doors closed tightly and the floor was covered in soft carpets and hand-woven rugs. The colours were muted and the lighting from the ceiling and on the tables was adjusted to be as inconspicuous as possible. Everything was designed to put the focus on the food. The waiters were elegant old men from whom both ego and aggressive masculinity had been removed like the bitterness from vegetables. They gave the impression of men who had driven themselves to ruin over food and had now mastered the art of taking their own pleasure in the pleasure of others. The meal was served with all the solemnity of a holy communion and the discretion of a secret rendezvous. In front of the table now was a bowl of pale yellow soup that seemed to reflect the clear sky of the early summer day. One of the old waiters appeared out of nowhere bearing a silver tray loaded with plates of beef bones cut into circles. With perfect timing he gave a slight nod and scooped out the marrow with a spoon. Then he carefully let it slide off the spoon and into the centre of soup. It was transparent and gelatinous, and like a young maiden's heart seen through a crystal, it seemed to float in the juices of youth. Translated into Japanese cuisine it was something like a broth made with the soft cheek meat of sea bream. The old waiter bowed reverently, took a few steps back, and stood waiting. As he did so he seemed to be offering a humble prayer that the customers would receive this heavenly nectar with pleasure. Of course the food was prepared with exquisite care and the service was flawless. From then on until the dessert every course was all that was good and beautiful, and they finished the meal amid cries of pleasure.

'But we were left with a slightly bad aftertaste, because we felt it would have been exactly the same for anyone.'

'I know it is uncomfortable for you to be praised face to face so I won't say much, but while there were some odd combinations in what you made for us today, your cooking struck me as utterly *sincere*.'

The woman came out with one unexpected comment after another. Besshirō had never heard anyone use the word 'sincere' when describing food. The hardships of his upbringing had made him a cynic, and he hated the very sound of words like 'sincere' or 'heartfelt'. If this were a quality he did have, he felt sure that he would be left as vulnerable as a new-born chickling, surrounded and taken advantage of by the insincere world. Frailty, thy name is *sincerity*. Was not the point of art that it rid one of such things and kept a person strong? That it made it possible to hold out against the lies and hypocrisy of others? Leave it to a *waka* poet to say such old-fashioned and disagreeable things. It was the kind of art criticism you would expect from a strait-laced schoolgirl. And he saw no reason to engage it. The couple's authority in Besshirō's eyes evaporated at this thought, and he felt his customary swagger returning.

'Ha, ha, ha, ha! "The cuisine of *sincerity*, is it?"'

A car came to pick them up and the couple said goodbye. When Besshirō asked them where they were going next they said they were going to worship at the Mibuji Temple and take in a performance of mimed Buddhist morality plays. He teased them, saying, 'That's perfect for a pious couple like yourselves.' But the woman knitted her brow and replied, 'Is that the way you see it? Actually we go there because the sound of the bells and the gongs makes us feel like we've come to listen to the music of hell.' Her husband the painter was annoyed by the irony in Besshirō's voice. 'You may think we're a couple of goody-two-shoes, but we've been through our share of hell. It's just that lately we've started to feel we've been taking up space in paradise for too long, so we're looking around for a seat in hell again. We weren't born yesterday, you know.' The woman tugged at her husband's elbow and said, 'Now you leave this beautiful young man alone. He's a work of art and you'll break him if you're not careful!' She seemed to find her own words amusing and burst out laughing as she got into the car.

Besshirō never saw the couple again after these two spring meetings, but they had swooped in on him like a tornado and destroyed the fortress he had built around himself. He had learned something about art from them. But he had no intention at this point in his life of getting involved in some musty old religion, and the idea of pursuing what the woman called *sincerity* seemed like cheap moralism and made him nauseous. All he needed was a way to find peace. And what besides death could really deliver that? It would come willy-nilly and erase everything. The trick was to find solace in that inevitability and do all you could to enjoy the life you have. If he could do this there could be no debate about the distinction between taste and art in what he created. 'If things get really bad I can always just die.' Since he was a child, whenever he found himself in a difficult place or things did not go his way he would wind up inescapably at this suffocating idea of Emptiness, which his young brain had elaborated into a proactive intellectual position. As if to certify the validity of his philosophy, the owner of the Maison Higaki's death provided a prime example right before his eyes.

About a year earlier his friend had noticed a cancerous growth on the left side of the back of his neck. At first it caused him no pain. The doctor said there was no need to remove it and treated it with X-rays instead. It got smaller at first but eventually swelled up larger than before. And then the pain started. At this point the doctor could no longer keep the truth from him and told him it was lung cancer that had broken to the surface. Higaki was not surprised when he heard this. 'There are still a few things I wanted to do but didn't get to. But I suppose I've done more than most people.' 'Time to wrap things up and pay the bill,' he said with a laugh and set about putting his affairs in order. Once he had sold the restaurant and taken care of all of his debts there was a little money left. Saying that he wanted to die somewhere lively, he moved to a back street in Kyōgoku. He hired a pretty nurse and his favourite model to be his companions until death. And then began to prepare what he called 'a genius's death'.

He decorated his room with the few items from his collection that he had been too fond of to sell, but even so it was as packed as the shop of a Jewish curio dealer. He installed his canopy bed, which of course was a fake, but which he claimed had been the possession of a Spanish nobleman who became a wandering minstrel and travelled to the United States during the Civil War. It did have poetry carved in Roman letters on its posts. He kept up his painting sitting upright in bed.

Sometimes the cancer became excruciatingly painful, too painful for oral painkillers. He begged the doctor for injections of morphine, but the latter rarely allowed it for fear that it would weaken him too much. His entire body turned black and blue and then the skin in the hollows around his protruding bones started to take on a light purple colour. He was just past middle age, but stooped over under the weight of the swollen tumour behind his neck he looked like a dwarf or a hungry ghost. It was the middle of summer and he was not wearing any clothes, so the miserable sight of him was on full display to send chills down the spine of whoever saw it. When the pain attacked him he would writhe and suffer in his nakedness. He was soaked in heavy sweat, as if someone had poured water over his entire body, and as he twisted and rubbed together his long thin limbs in a futile attempt to rid himself of the pain he looked like a snake in the throes of giving birth. They were very close, but Besshirō hated watching his friend suffer.

He had more pain in his own life than he could handle. And this sort of pain in particular, he felt, could easily stain his sensibilities. For an artist it was poison, and he wanted to avoid it as much as possible. So whenever Higaki started to feel pain, Besshirō would slip out of his sick room and go for a cup of tea or a chat. But his sick friend would not allow it. As he gasped for breath he said, 'Don't be a coward. I want you to watch this and see that it is actually quite thrilling once you've come this far.'

Besshirō squeezed his hand until it hurt and forced himself to watch as his entire body was drenched in the same heavy sweat. He was not afraid of death, although the thought did cross his mind that there were plenty of unpleasant things on the way there. This thought, however, began to subside as his friend's suffering grew worse. Something else began to emerge in Besshirō's mind as he grew numb from the sheer horror of the sight. Look at the thing writhing there. It is no longer a living creature. It is just an object that has long since been cut off from the breath of life, like a mummy excavated from the catacombs in Egypt or a desiccated corpse pulled from a cave in Tibet. The fact that it is still moving makes it seem like an ancient doll powered by an intricate mechanism beyond modern understanding. The doll is black and blue and pulsates with a consistent rhythm, twists and writhes, and suddenly sits bolt upright. Then it collapses and groans with what seems its last breath and the same sequence is repeated over and over. The horror of it was enough to make the model start crying. But then she found it funny and contorted her face into a strange expression as she peeked at him from behind her sleeve. The nurse looked angry as she fanned him with a paper fan.

Besshirō had figured it out. His sick friend was trying to enjoy the worst of his pain. He was adding a desperate rhythm to the natural writhing of his body against the pain to turn it into a kind of dance. Did this help him to deal with the pain? Or was his friend trying to show him what he had meant when he used to talk about 'the ultimate art'? He started his dance again, twisting and turning, grunting and groaning until he collapsed with a cry of anguish. He was imitating a Muslim in prayer, but he was doing it all in time with the sound of a third-rate band that could be heard from a nearby movie theatre.

Even more surprising was the fact that his friend had had a mirror placed on the opposite wall so he could enjoy the sight of his own pathetic dance. He had even placed a blue wall-hanging and a vase with summer flowers next to his bed so they would be reflected in the background. Besshirō was outraged. He lashed out at the model, 'Why are you letting him do this? He's a sick man!' 'He said he wanted to!' she protested. His friend gave him a reproachful look that said he shouldn't blame the girl.

When he got injections of morphine, which the doctor allowed once for every three times he asked, Higaki would be laughing and in high spirits. His appetite would return as well at those times and he would ask Besshirō to cook whatever he wanted.

The sorts of things he usually ate, such as *soupe a l'oignon* served baked in a small bowl covered in cheese, rice with stewed ox tongue, or salad with *haricots verts* and vinaigrette, were easy enough for Besshirō to prepare. But dishes like duck simmered in duck blood or eel medallions with vinegared aspic were new to Besshirō and more challenging to make even with the detailed instructions his friend would rattle off from his bed. Simmering the duck blood on an alcohol burner made a rich and sticky broth, like a good red-bean soup, in which the slices of duck were cooked along with salt and pepper. He tasted the meat after cooking it very lightly and was surprised to find that it did not taste bloody. His friend explained that it was the specialty of a famous duck restaurant in Paris and was considered quite an elaborate and extravagant dish. The eel medallions, on the other hand, were a lower-class dish that was sold on the streets in poor Italian immigrant neighbourhoods. It was not particularly good. But his friend seemed to be enjoying the memories attached to these foods and asked for one after another without properly eating any of them. When no wild duck could be found they would make do with small domesticated ones, and in late summer, when the peas were no longer edible, Besshirō ran around looking for springy string beans. When his friend became nostalgic for his childhood he asked for *monja-yaki* pancakes and roasted sweet potatoes.

Besshirō did everything he could to fulfil his friend's wishes. But sometimes the painkillers would still be working after the food had been cooked and enjoyed, and his friend would demand that he keep him company playing games, and even Besshirō's patience would start to run thin. Once he asked Besshirō to paint a human face in oils on the tumour on the back of his neck, which had grown to the size of a ball of yarn. He thought it would be hilarious to invite friends over and tell them he had grown another face. Besshirō refused, but his friend insisted so he reluctantly took up his brush. As he removed the bandages to reveal the lump of flesh, turned the colour of alligator skin from X-ray burns and ointment, it seemed to have a stubborn, anti-human will of its own. The tumour had a hard core that gave it a smooth round shape, with flesh stretched tight over it that made one want to stab it with a knife or gouge out its defiant hardness. The paint adhered well to the skin on the tumour. As Besshirō felt it through the paint on the end of his brush he understood how much his friend hated this stubborn lump, so much that he had to make a joke of it to be able to deal with it. 'Make it look like a guy who doesn't give a shit about pain.' Besshirō painted the base and started to paint a nose, mouth and eyes while his friend gritted his teeth in pain. But before long the pain was too much. 'Ow! Ow! Ow! ow ow ow!'

'I can't take it any more. That's enough. Just get somebody to finish the job on my dead body when I don't feel any more pain,' he said. As a result the face was left with only one eye. And it was off centre. Besshirō did not fix it when Higaki died.

98

The fake face on the tumour was looking hard at something with its one eye and laughing, and the arbitrary way it had slipped off centre seemed to have some deep significance. It was a face that watched over life's frustrations and the impermanence of worldly things. Why embellish it any further? Besshirō just gave one last look at the unfinished face that peeked out from over the shoulder of his friend's corpse, said, 'All right!' and closed the coffin before the whole thing was cremated.

The pain never let up and the injections continued. Higaki stopped being able to consume solid foods and spent all of his time gasping for breath in bed. Besshirō thought he looked like one of those stuffed seals in front of the seal merchants' shops at the night market, and was amazed at how much people's appearances can change. His friend stopped being able to swallow and his pain seemed to stop as well. The doctor announced that the end was near. The nurse and the model blinked away quiet tears as they began to prepare for the move back home. Often it was hard to tell if the patient was conscious or not. But Besshirō heard a sound coming from the back of his throat and when he put his ear up close, he could hear him singing. It was not a song that he had heard him sing before. But he listened very closely to the faint sound and could make out the nonsense syllables of a lullaby. '*Nen korori yo!, Nen korori, nen korori!*'

Higaki tried hard to smile when he realised that Besshirō had brought his face up next to his. And by piecing together the partial words that he was able to form, Besshirō understood that he was saying something like this. 'Everywhere I looked it was all cleaned out. There was nothing. Nothing to leave you to remember me by. But wait! I have an aunt in Tokyo. She's still around – not dead yet, and I can almost see her there in the distance. I'm leaving her to you. It'll be good. I'm giving her to you, so she's your aunt now.'

His friend died. Aside from the merchants he used to do business with at the restaurant and a few casual friends, he had no close relatives in Kyoto. Besshirō got in touch with the aunt in Tokyo, who said she was too old to travel and asked him to take care of all of the funeral arrangements. So Besshirō handled the cremation himself.

He brought the ashes with him to Tokyo. The former owner of the Maison Higaki had been born in Tokyo but had not been in contact with any of his family, although there was a family plot in a cemetery in Akasaka Aoyama. Besshirō brought the ashes there because Higaki had been the head of his family and his aunt wanted him buried there. Then he settled in at the woman's house in downtown Tokyo while he did some sight-seeing around Tokyo, intending to return to Kyoto after about a month. But after a month he had already become the captive of Higaki's aunt.

Mrs Higaki had made her start as a cooking instructor at a girls' school, and since it was still the early days of girls' schools she was also called upon to teach whatever else they needed that had to do with household management. Once the girls' schools became more rigorously academic these subjects were no longer taught and she was out of a job. But she managed to turn this situation to her own advantage by opening a private finishing school for brides-to-be in the *shita-machi*. Her family situation was quite sad: she had lost her husband early and then four children as well, leaving only one daughter, who had just reached marrying age and helped out at the school. She was an anaemic and timid young woman, constantly scolded and overworked by her mother. The students called her 'Miss' but it was clear they had no respect for her. She was the kind of woman who quaked with fear whenever anyone said a word to her.

Mrs Higaki had taken in Besshirō's friend when he was orphaned as a child and raised him as one of her own children. She said she had got pretty fed up with him when he left home and wandered around abroad for years at a time without ever writing. But now that he was gone, if she left things as they were there would be no one to carry on the family name.

Higaki's family had been the main branch and his aunt had married into a cadet branch of the Higaki family. She said she didn't care if her own family died out, but she wanted to do something to preserve the main line of the Higakis. So she wanted to know if Besshirō would marry her daughter, 'If you don't dislike her too much,' and name one of the children Higaki so that the family name at least would be reestablished. Then she would feel that she had done her duty towards the main branch of her family, and it would also be a lovely thing for Besshirō to do for his late friend. 'This daughter of mine is Higaki's only living cousin after all. That connection has to mean something.'

The first time Besshirō heard this proposal he just laughed it off. His friend's life had been a whirlwind dedicated to the arts and it had ended beautifully, like the moment when one realises the lingering reverberations of the music one has been listening to are in fact made of air and not the textured substance that they seemed to be. His aunt's proposal was far too pedestrian and mundane to do justice to the way Higaki had lived and died. No matter how you sliced it, this was not the way to carry on his legacy. And Besshirō was not in the least attracted to the daughter. Cradling his head in one hand, Besshirō looked flabbergasted. 'There's no way,' he said. But the aunt was not to be dissuaded.

'You should get yourself set up in Tokyo. It's a lovely city, you know,' she said, and, having sized up Besshirō's abilities, immediately began tying a few more anchors around his neck by getting him some odd jobs at the Keisetsu Villa and with three or four other important families. She was very close with the Araki family, having had the elder sister Ochiyo as a pupil in her finishing school.

She had no spunk and no character. And it was precisely this extraordinary mediocrity in Itsuko, the woman's youngest daughter and Higaki's cousin, that eventually ensnarled Besshirō. For someone like Besshirō, who had so many protruding thorns, a woman like Itsuko, who was soft as thin cotton, turned out to pose the greater risk of entanglement. Besshirō's fits of rage, which resulted from his frustrations towards other people, would eventually be translated into outrageous demands towards those closest to him. 'Yes, yes!' she would say, with a melancholy and always slightly surprised look on her face, and scurry off to do what he had asked. Her timidity made Besshirō feel that he was able to hurl lightning bolts, and he started to enjoy looking down on her as she tremblingly awaited his next command, never questioning how humiliating a role she was being asked to play. Too terrified even to utter a cry of pain, she took the full force of the abuse and scorn he heaped upon her in exchange for all the wrongs the world had done him. She had the advantage of fastidiousness. Her emotions were muted, cool, and weak. And she had an idiotic honesty that made it impossible even to be annoyed with her. Meanwhile, the aunt smiled faintly and kept up her efforts to persuade him. And much to Besshirō's surprise, Itsuko had soon become indispensable to him. They ended up just like a married couple, and Mrs Higaki got what she wanted. Besshirō settled down in Tokyo and decided to tell people that Itsuko was his younger sister. And from time to time he would marvel at the way things had followed the script laid out by his friend's last, delirious words, 'I'm giving her to you, so she's your aunt now!'

He had not forgotten the mother who had borne him back in Kyoto or the old man who had fed him until he was almost a young man. But in his current situation it was the very depth of the connection that made it painful to remember them. Although Mrs Higaki was the aunt of a very good friend, she was not a blood relation, and he found that casually calling her 'Auntie' was just about the right level of intimacy. He could ratchet it up or down as he liked and it did not weigh him down with responsibility, which was perfect for him now that he was burning with the desire to make a name for himself in this vast city. It was convenient to have an old woman take care of you who didn't impose too much responsibility in return. He did not like to think, however, that Higaki, who had devoted his entire life to pleasure, made a game out of death when it came, and seemed to have lived his live like a poem written on the fly, had left behind in his unconscious delirium a single worldly thread in which to entangle his friend, a thread that had proven surprisingly alive and significant.

Among the three or four powerful families that Higaki's aunt had introduced him to, Besshirō became most involved with the owner of the Keisetsu Villa.

Keisetsu was a born and bred Tokyoite and a scholar of Chinese who was no doubt a progressive thinker in his younger days. He gave lectures and wrote widely, wore Chinese suits made of oilcloth and attended conferences about Japan's policy towards the Asian continent. But his way of thinking was eventually deemed behind the times and then his wife was killed in suspicious circumstances, so he cut his ties to the world of government and went into business selling much sought after dictionaries of Chinese characters and study guides for entrance examinations. When these did well he bought a few houses and plots of land to rent and engaged in various other money-making schemes. He became quite a wealthy man.

Keisetsu lived as a widower. He took his older daughter Ochiyo out of finishing school and had her manage the household while he showered his affection on the younger Okinu. Partly as a result of his idiosyncrasies, this scholar-merchant's house had very few visitors aside from old connections like Mrs Higaki. From his very first visit Keisetsu thought of Besshirō as an incorrigible but stimulating monster. He could discuss just about anything having to do with the *koto*, *go*, calligraphy, or painting, and everything he said was barbed with contradictions that had Keisetsu passionately arguing with him before he knew it. When it came to food in particular, Besshirō would actually prepare dishes to prove his points. He had an uncanny understanding of the psychology of eccentrics that allowed him to memorise the tastes of this ageing gastronome and play his tongue like a piano keyboard. Being a widower, Keisetsu had plenty of time on his hands which he spent huffing and puffing in the blazing sun as if the fat in his body were on fire, wearing a pith helmet and torturing his potted plants, obsessing over his livestock and all manner of strange objects that he collected. Sometimes he would become crazed with fury and indignation at the world that had made him so much money only to accuse him of having sold out and thrown away the respect that he once had as a scholar. Partly in reaction to this grievance, Keisetsu's obsession with food became all the more intense.

Keisetsu made Ochiyo work like a housewife while he took enormous pleasure in buying the latest fashions for Okinu and sending her to a French Catholic school in a fancy neighbourhood. This was no doubt because Okinu was his favourite, but it was also typical of his tendency toward extremes. He had started to experiment with cooking snapping turtle before Besshirō arrived and had managed to make a passable hot pot out of it, but he had yet to succeed at steam baking it. Besshirō easily showed him how to prepare the hot coals in which to bury the live turtle wrapped in unbleached cotton, how to keep the temperature right, and how to know when it was ready. When it was done Keisetsu tore it apart, dunked it in soy sauce, and experienced a taste like nothing he had had in quite a while. Until then Besshirō had been going by the nickname Yoshirō, which he had been given in Kyoto, but once Keisetsu started to keep him around the older man substituted the character for 'snapping turtle' for the first character in 'Yoshirō' and rechristened him 'Besshirō'. His daughters followed suit and got used to calling him by this name as well. Keisetsu was a possessive man and wanted Besshirō all for himself, so he gave him and his wife a place to live and a small salary and forbade him from working for any other family.

From the first time he entered the Keisetsu Villa, Besshirō was smitten with Okinu. No woman could be further removed from the world he lived in and none could be so close to his ideal. She had an innocent look, as if she were always dreaming, accompanied by the slightest hint of bitterness. But she also exuded a kind of authority like that of crops picked at first harvest that yet hoard in some inaccessible place inside them the future growth they have been denied.

Okinu took little notice of the young man who had become part of their quiet household. Sometimes when she was next to him she would even forget he was there and abandon herself to solitary games and daydreams. Perhaps because she had lost her mother and been brought up by a proud father, at these times she exuded a sort of unfeminine and dignified loneliness. She seemed oblivious to Besshirō's good looks. It was Ochiyo who would blush and fidget when she saw him.

When Besshirō was in Okinu's presence he could not help showing off and being even more overbearing than usual. She would lift her usually downcast eyes and look the young man straight in the eye, almost as if she could see straight through to his heart. This made Besshirō feel utterly out of his league and his heart ached with his own commonness.

But along with his duties as Keisetsu's companion, Besshirō had been instructed to teach the sisters how to cook, and once he had Okinu in his hands as his pupil, he became more at ease. Her cooking skills were as untutored and clumsy as any normal girl's and as adorable as the white skin that peeked out from the split seams in her kimono. He was able to enjoy her foibles at his leisure while he scolded and cursed. Okinu was unfazed and always answered back, but she did seem to have gained some respect for this young man's extraordinary skills. Besshirō felt encouraged and spoke about his theories of art, taking the opportunity to brag as he did so. He stopped feeling hesitant around her. But that was all there was to their relationship. Just as he was thinking how much he liked this girl, Besshirō continued to trudge along in his humdrum family life with Itsuko. Soon he had a child as well and Mrs Higaki was eagerly awaiting the next one, who was meant to take the Higaki name.

Tonight, inspired by the sticky darkness of the foggy night, Besshirō decided to indulge himself in a rare moment of reflection on the life he had led up until then. He had sought solace in the thought of death as an absolute that would settle everything, and then looked back from that void on his brief life to see how trivial it was. Having reached that point, he was able to look at death itself and see it also as something light and insubstantial. He had elaborated these ideas into his own philosophy and lived by it from the time of his childhood until now.

And yet he had grown increasingly sceptical of the possibility of making the best of the time one has and giving free rein to one's desires. He had not been able to realise a single one of his desires. Even the art of cooking, which he had pursued consistently, was tangled up in worldly matters and seemed to have become like a lever that controlled him and pushed him in unexpected directions.

The hail was falling in the deep and inky darkness. The white pellets were swallowed up by the blackness as they fell and yet they kept on falling as if they might finally whiten the night.

It was late and the neighbouring houses were completely silent, with only the occasional rumble of a train passing by on the main street. His wife seemed to have fallen asleep in the next room, but from time to time when the baby was about to cry she would quieten him by whispering, 'Daddy's here. Daddy's here,' and pressing her breast to his face, after which she would continue to breathe softly in her sleep. For the first time tonight Besshirō felt pity for his little son, who had already learned to choke back his tears when he heard his mother say this to avoid the wrath of his moody father. His own father had told his mother to tell him he hadn't asked to be born either if his son ever complained about being brought into this world, and as he thought back on that tonight it seemed like a conclusion his father had reached only after a great deal of thought. Now Besshirō's son too was saddled with a fate that he did not understand.

Besshirō's father had brought him into the world without understanding why, saying, 'I didn't ask for this either,' and now Besshirō was doing the same to his son. His mother, who had conveyed his father's message, was brought to the temple to expiate the sins of her own father and had managed to free herself of all desires except the desire for food. She regretted this, but still passed that desire on to her son. He remembered how when as a boy he was invited to eat with other families, she would insist on hearing about the food in the most minute detail and then look as content as if she had eaten it herself. His only friend Higaki, whom he cared for until he died, had unconsciously set a trap for Besshirō on his deathbed so that he would marry his cousin and produce an heir to take his family name. All of this reminded him that nothing in this world is over in a single generation. There was nothing that he felt he had accomplished alone. It was the same for everyone. Like his father had said, we were all entangled with each other. He had first realised this when he met that painter and his poet wife that spring in Kyoto. '... We've been taking up space in paradise for too long so we're looking around for a seat in hell again,' they had said. Was this their way of saying that they recognised that this inevitable entanglement with others would cast them out of paradise eventually? Did that mean that this idea of sincerity that the woman had spoken of was not some cheap moralism after all, but something much trickier that flowed from deeper sources? What was it then?

The night wore on and the sticky liquid darkness deepened. Insatiably it devoured the hail from below as it fell. Looked at another way, it seemed to be spitting it down from above. Eating and spitting, spitting and eating, the darkness was never satisfied. Besshirō had never known such a powerful appetite. Was this what the one looked like who devoured death and spat out life?

He gave himself up to the darkness and found it bewitching as he stared into it. He felt something soft and lush that seemed to toy with his heart. Okinu? Could it be? Or is it some trick?

The daikon hotpot had boiled down and the bottom looked like a garbage-strewn beach at low tide. He went to the kitchen and found several bottles of beer that the boy from the liquor store must have delivered. These he brought into the main room and decided, even though he was not much of a drinker, that he would spend the night drinking and watching the hail. But *daikon* wouldn't do as an accompaniment to this insatiable darkness.

He called out gently to the next room.

'Itsuko, would you mind going to wake them up at Izu-shō and see if they have some monkfish liver or filefish liver? They'll let you have it if you tell them that Sensei wants it.'

For once he asked politely. 'Yes, Yes,' she answered sleepily. As he listened to the sound of Itsuko's footsteps as she hurried out, he added some coals to the brazier. When the fifty-candle-power bulb shone on his sideways leaning face, a drop of liquid sparkled in Besshirō's eye that had never been seen before.

Glossary

Ebi imo: A traditional Kyoto vegetable. Literally 'shrimp potatoes', so named because they are curved like a shrimp.

Four Arts: The four arts that, according to Chinese tradition, were considered obligatory for gentlemen scholars. They include the *koto* (Chinese *qin*), *go*, calligraphy, and painting. Each of these is expressed with one Chinese character, constituting a four-character expression (*kin-gi-sho-ga*) the collective meaning of which is something like 'the polite arts'.

Go: A complex board game using black and white stones placed on a grid. Players try to capture each other's stones and occupy larger spaces on the board. The game originated in China but is most popular in Japan.

Hakama: A square-shaped apron-like divided skirt that is tied at the waist and worn over a kimono.

Hōraimame: Sugar-coated beans popular in Kyoto. Their name means 'wealth-bringing beans'.

Ichiraku kimono: A kimono with a diagonal pattern woven directly into the silk.

Kaguya-hime: A fairy princess in the tenth-century narrative *Taketori monogatari* (*The Tale of the Bamboo Cutter*). Born from a piece of bamboo and raised by an old bamboo cutter and his wife, she grows to become a matchless beauty but refuses all proposals of marriage, even from the Emperor himself, and eventually ascends back to heaven.

Kaiseki: A meal consisting of numerous small and simple dishes often served with the tea ceremony but also considered a form of haute cuisine, especially in Kyoto. The emphasis is on taste, presentation, and the freshness of ingredients.

Kara-age: Japanese-style fried chicken.

Kokyū: A Japanese three-stringed musical instrument played with a bow.

Koto: A Japanese musical instrument like a large zither with thirteen strings that are plucked using finger picks. It is played from a seated position. Skill at the koto was once a crucial skill for geisha and samurai women.

Magemono: Round boxes made by bending thin pieces of cypress wood that have been made flexible by heating or soaking in hot water.

Monja-yaki: A popular dish in Kyoto and Osaka made at the table with batter and various ingredients. It is similar to *okonomi-yaki*, which is more popular in Tokyo, but the batter in *monja-yaki* is more runny.

Obasuteyama: Remote mountaintops where poor villagers were said to leave old women to die when they became too much of a burden.

Ogiebushi: A quiet and contemplative style of shamisen playing developed by Ogie Royu in the eighteenth century and related to the *nagauta* style. Once popular among Yoshiwara geisha, it is now one of the three styles designated *kokyoku* or 'old styles' and has been recognised since 1993 as an intangible national treasure. The example sung by Mataichi's adoptive father in *A Riot of Goldfish* makes use of a common pun on the words for 'to wait' and 'pine tree', both of which are read *matsu*.

Ono no Komachi (*c.* 825 – *c.* 900): a Heian-period poet known for her beauty and for playing hard to get. The 'Seven Komachis' in *A Riot of Goldfish* refer to the seven plays in the repertoire of the Noh theatre that tell her story.

Oribako: A box made by folding together thin pieces of wood or thick paper. Typically they do not use fasteners.

Rakugo: A form of comic monologue in which a single performer plays the roles of multiple characters. For the duration of the performance the storyteller remains seated Japanese-style on a mat using only a fan and a small cloth for props and limited but dramatic gestures for emphasis.

Shakuhachi: A bamboo flute. The name refers to its length: one *shaku* and eight (*hachi*) *sun*, or about 55 centimetres.

Shita-machi: The areas of Tokyo such as Asakusa, Kanda, and Nihonbashi, that originally lay outside the boundaries of Edo castle. It is associated with Edo commoner culture, the plebeian 'downtown' to the 'uptown' known as Yamanote. In 'The Food Demon' the wealthy Araki family lives in Yamanote and Besshiro lives in the Shita-machi.

Shōji: A sliding door made with paper glued to a wooden latticework.

Tatami: Rectangular straw mats used for flooring in traditional Japanese houses. They are made in a uniform size (although the precise measurements differ by region) so the number of mats may be used to indicate the size of a room. A six-mat room in Tokyo is 9.3 square metres while in Kyoto it is just under eleven square metres.

Tempyō era: 724–794 AD. Era in the late Nara period when Japan was actively adopting Tang Chinese and Buddhist culture. It is known for an efflorescence of sophisticated and realistic Buddhist sculpture.

Tokonoma: An alcove in a traditional Japanese house used for the display of ornamental objects such as hanging scrolls or vases.

Wabi: An aesthetic of extreme simplicity associated with the tea ceremony and deriving from the Buddhist idea of impermanence.

Waka: A 31-syllable classical Japanese poem. Also known as *tanka* (short poem). Okamoto Kanoko was an accomplished *waka* poet before she became a novelist.

Biographical note

Kanoko Okamoto (1889–1939) was born into a wealthy family in what is now the Minato Ward of Tokyo. She began to contribute *tanka* poetry – a classical Japanese style – to a periodical while still a high school student, and went on to publish four volumes of verse. She met her husband, the caricaturist Ippei Okamoto, in 1908, and they were married two years later. Their first child, Tarō Okamoto, was born a year later, and went on to become a famous avant-garde artist. Their two younger children, a girl and then a boy, both died in infancy. These grievances and other deaths in her immediate family caused Okamoto to turn to religion, and she would ultimately write several essays on her chosen faith of Buddhism.

After publishing her fourth volume of poetry, Okamoto decided to turn her hand to fiction, and moved her family to Europe in 1929 with a view to pursuing this end. They visited Paris, London and Berlin before touring the United States, and returned to Japan in 1932. Soon after, she published her first fictional work, the novella *Tsuru wa Yamiki* (*The Dying Crane*). She went on to publish several more works of prose fiction before dying of a brain haemorrhage in 1939, at the age of just forty-nine.

HESPERUS PRESS

Hesperus Press, as suggested by the Latin motto, is committed to bringing near what is far – far both in space and time. Works written by the greatest authors, and unjustly neglected or simply little known in the English-speaking world, are made accessible through new translations and a completely fresh editorial approach. Through these classic works, the reader is introduced to the greatest writers from all times and all cultures.

For more information on Hesperus Press, please visit our website: **www.hesperuspress.com**

ET REMOTISSIMA PROPE

NEW AND FORTHCOMING TITLES
FROM HESPERUS WORLDWIDE

Author	Title	Foreword writer
Eduardo Belgrano Rawson	*Washing Dishes in Hotel Paradise*	
Buddhadeva Bose	*My Kind of Girl*	
Bankim Chandra Chatterjee	*The Forest Woman*	
Shiro Hamao	*The Devil's Disciple*	
Rabindranath Tagore	*Boyhood Days*	Amartya Sen

SELECTED TITLES FROM HESPERUS PRESS

Author	Title	Foreword writer
M. Ageyev	*A Romance with Cocaine*	Toby Young
Mary Borden	*The Forbidden Zone*	Malcolm Brown
Rupert Brooke	*Letters from America*	Benjamin Markovits
Anthony Burgess	*The Eve of St Venus*	
Ivy Compton-Burnett	*Pastors and Masters*	Sue Townsend
Walter de la Mare	*Missing*	Russell Hoban
E.M. Forster	*The Obelisk*	Amit Chaudhuri
Graham Greene	*No Man's Land*	David Lodge
L.P. Hartley	*The Brickfield*	
Aldous Huxley	*After the Fireworks*	Fay Weldon
Mikhail Kuzmin	*Wings*	Paul Bailey
Jack London	*The People of the Abyss*	Alexander Masters
Klaus Mann	*Alexander*	Jean Cocteau
Luigi Pirandello	*Loveless Love*	
Vita Sackville-West	*The Heir*	
Leonardo Sciascia	*A Simple Story*	Paul Bailey
Frank Wedekind	*Mine-Haha*	
Edith Wharton	*Fighting France: from Dunkerque to Belfort*	Colm Tóibín
Leonard Woolf	*A Tale Told by Moonlight*	Victoria Glendinning
Virginia Woolf	*Memoirs of a Novelist*	
Yevgeny Zamyatin	*We*	Alan Sillitoe